ANIMAL TRUTH

Animal Truth and Other Stories
Copyright © 2022 by Sharona Muir. All rights reserved.
ISBN: 978-1-60801-238-1

Library of Congress Cataloging-in-Publication Data

Names: Muir, Sharona, 1957- author.
Title: Animal truth and other stories / Sharona Muir.
Description: New Orleans, Louisiana : University of New Orleans Press,
   [2022]
Identifiers: LCCN 2022021775 (print) | LCCN 2022021776 (ebook) | ISBN
   9781608012381 (paperback ; acid-free paper) | ISBN 9781608012398 (ebook)

Subjects: LCGFT: Short stories.
Classification: LCC PS3552.E5355 A83 2022 (print) | LCC PS3552.E5355
   (ebook) | DDC 813/.54--dc23/eng/20220504
LC record available at https://lccn.loc.gov/2022021775
LC ebook record available at https://lccn.loc.gov/2022021776

First edition.
Printed in the United States of America on acid-free paper.

UNIVERSITY OF NEW ORLEANS PRESS
2000 Lakeshore Drive
New Orleans, Louisiana 70148
unopress.org

ANIMAL TRUTH

and other stories

SHARONA MUIR

For my mother,
in loving memory

CONTENTS

MENU: EXTINCTION

The young artist's wife had begun smelling strange, lately. He was sure of it, and her odors perplexed him because she wouldn't admit to them, but only joked and teased when he tried to probe.

"You're sure you're not snacking on something? Cheese? Pickles? Or could there be a change in your hormones or skin chemistry?"

Weren't pregnant women driven to eat odd things? In Cambridge, Massachusetts you could buy anything. He imagined strange viands, bottles with arcane labels, half-hydrated roots, reeking, tucked into the recesses of the kitchen cabinets where he thrust his stretched-out fingers that brushed only cobwebs and dead moths. He waited till she was out, then interrogated her dresser drawers as well as the steamer trunk and the bathroom's medicine cabinet: nothing. Their tenth-floor studio in the married students' dormitory lacked hiding places. The room was shaped like a pie wedge, the wide end being a single panoramic window overlooking a city of brick, a river, and low-flying gulls. They had two computer desks of the cheapest description, a sofa-bed partly covered by a kilim, and lots of empty beige carpet. Their dining set comprised two chrome chairs and a formica table inherited from the university and dating back to the Atomic Age; it was the butt of cozy jokes, dear to them as only an ugly trysting-place can be to a couple in love, sitting together. Their wide window—never curtained—showed a night sky dominated by a neon sign that towered up across the river dividing Cambridge from Boston. The sign cycled through its performance in a minute: *Coca-Cola* came gradually into view, as if the name were a hollow tube filling from the bottom with bright red light until it glowed solid; then it blinked, reappeared in encore, and dissolved into a white foam that whirled round the letters and faded into blackness . . . a blackness against which his eyes insisted on seeing a faint, neuro-ophthalmic *Coca-Cola* where the real one would, shortly, continue its cycle. The couple were as fond of the sign as a country pair might have been of a mulberry tree shading their house and splattering it with berries.

In the nighttime, the room's walls flushed and paled; over the old chrome chairs and battered aluminum tea kettle glided a momentary candy glaze; the beige carpet reddened and sizzled with fuzzy luminosity. On their bed, the young artist's wife was a spectacle of cherry-tipped breasts casting ruddy shadows, of brown hair glinting like flame, of thighs bloodied with transparence, of eyes reflecting a dazzled pallor. Tracing her spine, as she lay against him, he saw its groove flow red, then white. As she neared term, the gaudy pattern of the monumental sign painted her swollen body with strange poignancy, as though the essence of their time together, of this early life, were stroking their baby from outside with hands of passing light.

He adored her. But she smelled wrong.

*   *   *

"Don't you want to check with your doctor if you're eating anything unusual?" By daylight, she was a medium-sized brunette, rather pear-shaped even before pregnancy. Her chin dipped into her neck and out again, with a gulp of amusement that raised her lovely eyebrows. Her short-nailed scholar's hands rested on his chest.

"*Come away sweet love and play thee, lest grief and care betray thee,*" she sang, clear as a wren; then lifted, with effort, her book bag and slung it over her shoulder, where it hung awkwardly off her maternity dress. "Nobody in the group says I have B.O." She ran a madrigal group; she was getting her master's degree in musicology and had a flair for arcana.

"It isn't B.O.," he protested, "you just smell like . . ."

"What."

"Some incredibly weird curry. Is Jamshed feeding you his left-overs?"

"No, silly, if he did I'd share them with you. But. Maybe we shouldn't eat at Jamshed's all the time. Maybe there's a clove up your nose." She kissed his nose and left.

They had eaten weeknights at Jamshed's since arriving in Cambridge. Jamshed, the director of a digital fabrication labo-ratory, was the artist's collaborator. He believed in the alliance of the arts and sciences to defeat the global forces of ignorance and greed; he believed that if you mixed the arts and sciences together, they created the glorious combustible thing called truth. He had brought the artist here, to the lab that he ran, which was funding and producing the artist's project, an installation called *Menu: Extinction.* It was to take the form of a grand banquet, cel-ebrating—in a spirit of black irony—humanity's power to extin-guish other species. There would be a table recalling the Last Supper, and a series of sculptures representing dishes. Each dish would serve up, elaborately cooked, the last member of an en-dangered species—the very last of its kind. Beside each offering would lie a menu, turned to the page describing it. The banquet's sinister cuisine would, of course, have a chef. What sort of chef, he had asked himself, would write that menu? Who would glory in serving up the last animal of an endangered species? The artist and his wife agreed that the chef would write with casual wit and nasty self-satisfaction, the style of the devil himself.

"He's Pico," she mused. "Who said that man is unique among the animals. But Pico gone horribly wrong—like, man is unique because he can eat all the animals." These plans had excited him, yet the artist's first attempts were one long stumble. For weeks, on paper and with digital aid, he conjured scores of en-dangered animals—spiny anteaters, silky sifakas, hirolas and addax. Hooves, horns, snouts, plumes. They fascinated him, but when he'd tried to compose the banquet scene, it flopped. Some-thing crucial was missing. The mock-ups of *Menu: Extinction* kept resembling nothing so much as a prank in a natural history mu-seum, or a severely misguided theme restaurant. The lab crew

liked every one of the mock-ups: they saw the logical outcome
of the project proposal. They were engineers. The artist saw the
failure of his imagination.

Then a breakthrough came.

One evening in late October, the artist and his wife had entered the elevator outside their apartment door and headed down
two floors, speculating as usual about how their bachelor host
had gotten to live in a married dorm. They found Jamshed in an
irate mood, kicking with his small Nike'd foot at some torn envelopes heaped in the middle of his beige carpet, which was even
emptier than theirs. The room held only a beanbag chair that he
slept in, some tenuous lamps, and a priceless, black mahogany,
Chinese-Victorian settee carved with writhing grotesques, which
had somehow followed him from the family estate in Mumbai
and was abundantly littered with papers. The Coca-Cola sign
was in its ruby phase, rouging Jamshed's round cheeks puffed
with indignation. With thumb and forefinger he plucked papers
from the settee and hoisted them like bits of soiled laundry. He
rattled the papers, which—they learned—were marriage applications sent by his aunts in the hope that he would interview a
suitable girl or two.

"This one speaks French. Should I take this one? What about
these ones?" He hurled the applications in the air and blew at
them, like wishing on a dandelion. They floated down through
the Coca-Cola sign's white carbonate strobe, while the artist's
wife laughed.

"You don't have to marry them, do you?"

Jamshed turned on them his black eyes, fringed with curly
lashes and unusually moist, the eyelids naturally stained purple
as though his ancestral line had lost sleep.

"Damn right," he grated. "I'm sorry. This really bugs me.
Come sit down. I don't need a wife anyway. Look at how I cook."

He had prepared a delectable, conversation-quelling dinner.
The couple ate with gusto, yet, seated by his wife at a different
formica table spattered with butter-drops, the artist felt her con-
straint. He felt the indelicacy of touching her shoulder, or lifting

a hair that dropped near her lips to tuck it behind her ear. And she would not pat his knee or nudge his foot. Their host's rawness dictated it. They tried to hide what Jamshed, so likeable, was excluded from unfairly. The whole game (the artist thought) of getting someone to love was unfair. To a sensitive man like Jamshed, the game was so high-stakes, and so uncontrollable, that he would naturally want to leave the table, but the table had animal legs and followed you around.

Perhaps the tension of keeping his hands from their tender habits was the triggering factor, the friction needed to strike a match in the artist's mind at the moment when his wife, turning a lump of apricot-glazed meat around on her fork, asked,

"What kind of meat is this?"

"What do you think?" twinkled Jamshed. "Maybe it is owl." There were rumors of an owl loose in the dorm; his wife wagged the unidentified lump and hooted, sounding more like a primate than a bird; and the artist said involuntarily,

"That's the problem."

He told them, there at the crowded, messy, redolent table. An animal on a plate was meat. Intellectually, you could deplore the sight of the last dodo's drumsticks, but at a primal level you were thinking, 'Yummy drumsticks.' That was why *Menu: Extinction* wasn't working. Nobody was moved at the primal level—the one that counted—by the sight of animals on plates. It was foolish.

"But . . . I thought . . . it worked," protested Jamshed, chewing. His wife lifted her chin, adorned with a shiny, fried crumb.

"Suppose I ask you to imagine," said the artist, "a mermaid. The last mermaid in the world. As an entrée in *Menu: Extinction*. A baked mermaid, prepared, à la Julia Child, with her tail obtruding from her open mouth, and her little fried fingers presented on a mother-of-pearl comb. How would that strike you?"

His wife blinked, then said that it struck her as perfectly horrid. Which was perfect.

*   *   *

After that evening, the *Menu: Extinction* team set out to fill the banquet plates with imaginary animals, the last members of their imaginary species: the last phoenix, the last Pegasus, the last clutch of dragon hatchlings, all done in the high cuisine of past centuries, the royal dishes prepared for the jaws of crowned heads, those symbols of humanity's might. The artist felt happy and energized; he slept well and rose eager for work. He laughed as he wrote the chef's menu copy: *A Chinese legend says that if you trap a mermaid, she will cry pearls until you release her—but, the legend warns, only an evil person would trap a mermaid. This charmingly expresses life's choices. You can be good and do without pearls. Or you can relish my sensational sirène enragée, a never-to-be-repeated delicacy celebrating your unique individual experience of fine dining and the good things in life!* . . . Everything went along as smoothly as could be, with the sole exception of the fact—the obstinate conundrum—of the artist's wife having begun to smell.

It was in January when, at his wife's suggestion, they stopped dining at Jamshed's for a short period. Still, she smelled of seared meats, brine, and pungent aromatics; of stewed fruits, savories, vinegars, and malts; of edible roots, fungi, and grapefruit peel.

"Nobody else says that I smell, and I have asked," she sighed, giving his buttock a sneaky pinch as he shaved. "You've got, like, psychosomatic hyper-nosmia, or something." Maybe she was right, he thought. A new baby, a new project; one might reasonably surmise that his nose registered the phantom smells of internal stress. When all this was over (vaguely, he meant the pregnancy and/or the project) he would go to a doctor. He'd never felt healthier, or happier, though, and inwardly protested that to contract an exotic psychic disorder was alien to his body, his character, and his history. As for other people's opinions, well, it put a man in a very awkward spot to have to ask his friends if they thought his wife smelled strange.

"It's not so great to keep telling me I stink," she announced one night. Her back was turned to him, her profile blued by the computer screen and her bare swollen feet, on the carpet to either side of her chair, bleached by the Coca-Cola sign to a fish-white puffiness. He saw her shoulders, unapproachable. The studio darkened as the neon sign re-started. Her remark had come out of nowhere, and he realized the gross humiliation of having given his wife a memorable hurt. The very next day he bought her a bouquet of stargazer lilies and sweetheart roses, a hugely expensive armful. The apology made them festive; they dressed for dinner and ate at a good restaurant; they came home and made love. The bouquet scented the studio, and the lilies' fleshy fragrance reassured him, while they lasted.

*   *   *

The pageant of the January snows, to which the holiday glamour clung, gave way to February's inhuman and violent storms that made their building quiver. The view from the wide window showed a baggy sky and a river like cement. Outside, in streets transformed into wind tunnels, their eyes streamed tears that their numbed faces didn't feel. In that obliterating cold, no smells survived except the noxious diesel of a passing truck or bus. The artist found himself savoring the weird flavors of his wife's neck, contrasts shouting of a warmer life, as he nuzzled into the scents of pickled limes and burnt dough, fermented hay and coffee grounds. . . .

Menu: Extinction's public opening was slated for early March. The installation looked great, and the artist trusted that it would bring his family—in March the baby was due!—some money as well as the recognition he craved. He was very tired, a blessing in disguise; otherwise he might have been nervous. The night before *Menu: Extinction* opened, he and Jamshed spent a couple of hours tossing back shots at a local bar. He got home just before midnight. He undressed, crept into bed and cuddled his big-bellied spouse, who kept drowsing off. He let her sleep, one arm over the blankets that rose and sank. The apartment was overheated, the air dry; the Coca-Cola sign's white burst was like static. He leaned into the small cloud of her breath, and sniffed her cheek: oily old lilies—no, saltier—whiff of untinned sardines. . . . All at once his limbs rebelled against the point-lessness of sleep; it had nothing to do with him. He forsook the bed and stood naked at the wide window. Far below, the thawed river was a winding rift in which columns of lights hung. The familiar dance of the Coca-Cola sign was twinned in the black deep. Farther upriver, a greenish smudge showed where the university's Great Dome hovered above Cambridge, lit up like the moon. He imagined its Doric portico in the floodlights, a row of fossil tusks under the grandiloquent brain-case of the Dome that symbolized the brilliant activities going on beneath it, in the long gut of the university's corridors. . . . Dozens of people were awake, now, working in their labs. He needed his work: the installation called him. Dressing hurriedly, on tiptoe, he watched as he closed the door, slowly, to make sure that his wife slept on undisturbed.

He used the palm-lock to enter. Nobody was in the main lab space, off which the art gallery extended through sliding doors. There was dim ambient light from monitors on equip-ment tables. Months of work were emerging in a final shape that seemed imminent yet far away, like the birth of his child. He unzipped his parka, tore loose the Velcro tabs on his gloves, loud rips in the semidarkness; he paused, having felt, more than heard, someone walking behind him—some lab tech on an all-night project? Nothing. Stuffing gloves into pockets, he walked to the gallery entrance and saw that his crew had set up the blood sacrifice. The sliding doors were open: in the doorway hung floor-length streamers of butcher paper bathed by a blood-red spotlight from inside. To his left, a blue-glazed ceramic "font" proffered rubber steaks in a dark fluid. Biting his lip, the artist picked up one of the rubber steaks, squeezed; it felt raw and moist. He wanted every visitor to feel symbolically part of that sacred slaughter, which brought people together and defined their roles, by inclusion and exclusion: king, priest, citizen, woman, foreigner, slave. . . . Still holding the rubber meat, he pressed it to a paper streamer, and saw a stamped human hand. Yeah, he was right to have come here early, in the dreaming hours, to check it all out, but really to revel in the unspeakably delicious pleasure of tumbling headlong down his own hard-earned rabbit hole. . . . The artist rotated, pupils widening with a stretch he could nearly feel, to absorb the melting and re-forming green-blue, yellow-tan, black-lime. . . . He'd composed this video stream of endangered species' images morphing into one another like a molten safari, ringed toes and plated nostrils, striped eyeballs and iridescent feathers and shaking, fringed lips and acid-blue eyes and eyes like faceted hematite, like evolution happening before him, flowing, melting, reforming, luminous as a summer's dream, across the four walls of the exhibit. Wherever he turned (he was turning around slowly) there were dewy gaz-es that shimmered into fulminous undersea worms; shocks of spines and wavy fur stared at him out of unspeakable grimaces. The walls were a magical bestiary come to life.

He saw the bubble forming, a white hole in the tapestry, to rep-resent extinction. Now other bubbles were entering the stream, expanding and popping circles of blankness. Now the bubbles were inseparable from the stream, a leprous effervescence that was bound to mess with everybody's nerves. He felt anxious him-self. Perfect!

He turned to the banquet table. The walls' aquatic light changed the banquet into a sort of shadowy coral reef; the figures that he'd created were gathered there, in the brooding mystery of completion; he felt a flutter as he picked out the details of their silhouettes and gleaming surfaces. The head of Pegasus staring into the four sauce-boats of its hooves. The Lamb of Gold, fleece aglitter, upright on its hind legs . . . He couldn't read the menus in which his own calligraphy, laser-etched on simulated rare woods, conveyed the words of the evil chef. And the major figures of the feast sprouted deformities that, under his fingertips, turned out to be shadows. . . .

He might have left. He might have returned to the sighing wife who couldn't get enough rest, with the weight of genera-tion planted in a spot that prevented her from sleeping soundly. He might have gone home to her. He might have rubbed his straining eyes, shrugged, and walked out of the gallery before the impression—more felt than heard—of footsteps began again behind him.

"Hey!" he called, looking into the rush of images that would have camouflaged anything (they were, after all—the animals—adept at camouflage). Must be a ventilation duct, he thought, turning back to the table. A whispering began.

Ignoring it, he stretched his hand toward a spectacular, three-foot-high, gelatinous column, with an Ionic capital that resembled colliding snails. The Galantine aux Petits Dragons—the flock of the last dragon hatchlings, small miracles of resin, paint, sugges-tion—served up in one of those great Baroque jellied salads that had really been filled with whole flocks of birds and schools of fish. A dainty dish to set before a king. The thing looked actually wet. He touched it.

It was wet.

"What the fuck," he muttered, sniffing his fingertips. They smelled like brine, aspic. . . . The artist felt a jolt go through his entire body. He came completely alert, yet felt trapped in a dream; he touched the Galantine again. It, faintly, quivered. Which it could not do. A column of solid resin? No. While his mind shrieked about pranks, last-minute novelties, his mouth took the measure of the situation and went dry.

He'd heard of mouths going dry; it had never happened to him. His tongue was cotton. He was beside the mermaid, her hair, braided strings of brown freshwater pearls, her eyes popping around the impediment of her great forked tail, pulled out from her grotesquely stretched mouth. Onions, celery, white wine, garlic, fennel, lemon, capers, pepper, verjuice, charcoal, singed flesh . . . He smelled the baked tail, he touched the elastic give of its scales. . . . The artist wiped his hands frantically on his jeans. Took a deep breath, held it, turned around. He began to walk away from his creation with the tread of a man venturing out on a frozen pond, not sure of its ability to sustain his weight. The banquet's smells overwhelmed him—it was as if he were walking away from the devil's kitchen.

Together with his feet, his mind stepped slowly, with extreme caution, over the surface of its sanity. Together, mind and body reached the butcher-paper veil, crossed the low red beam of light. As he parted the paper strands he saw, on the wall, a single white bubble his own height, with legs and arms and a fraying head, half-human, half candle-flame. It wiggled along the wall, a flat ghost mirroring him. He heard the whispers again, but they sounded . . . they sounded like sniggers.

He ducked through the butcher-paper veil, back into the main lab area where nobody was around, but his back insisted that footsteps followed him. He walked out, feeling followed, into the long gray corridor, the gut of the university, nicknamed the infinite corridor.

When he reached the infinite corridor, he began to run.

*   *   *

The dormitory elevator emitted a chime at each floor it reached. The artist, eyes shut, offered a wordless prayer for each chime. His knees were trembling. He had turned into one compact yearning for his wife, who was just a couple of elevator stops away. He wouldn't wake her. But he would tell her—he started framing words, words to tell her. That now he knew what evil was. That he'd summoned the evil chef in laughter and folly and arrogance, because he was after the glorious combustible thing called truth and he'd thought that protected him. But it didn't. How evil was impersonal and didn't care about his laudable intentions. How evil was also incredibly personal, and when you summoned evil, it split you so you didn't know yourself, it became the thing that held your parts together, tricked you into thinking you were whole. That he'd been a fool, he'd been a reckless idiot, he had sat the core of human evil to its portrait. But it was done, over, and all to the good, and he loved her, loved her, loved her.

The elevator chimed for the tenth floor. It was almost dawn. He gripped his right hand with his left hand to steady his key in the lock. The studio apartment was bathed in the Coca-Cola sign's fullest red glow, that glow that had often reminded him of a hearthfire. In the bed, his wife lay under mounded blankets as she had when he'd closed the door, a few hours earlier. With the clairvoyance of memory, he saw that she lay in the same, but the exact same, position. Immobile. As the artist caught his breath, he recognized the stench of carrion.

THE BATH OF VENUS

I chose a time too beautiful to share. I chose to float, and as extravagant as the idea seemed from the beginning, like all dreams it was ground beneath the millstone of details. During my first day away, I remained haunted by tasks left undone, fatal gaps in efficiency; but by sundown, I had accepted what was accomplished, and "away" lost its meaning. I must be home, since there was nowhere else to be.

Yes, I was afloat in beauty. My name for this new home was the Bath of Venus. Naturally, I hadn't called it that when I'd made the ruinously expensive arrangements that had transported me back in time nearly half a billion years. The sort of men who conduct research for private gain, in a certain style of hi-tech, clubby anarchy, have little more acquaintance with Venus than they have with doubt.

Under my houseboat deck rocked the gentle sea. Overhead, the sunset—growling from sea-rim to sea-rim with the fury of volcanic isles, far distant—sank into a dark depth of pastel stars. Ridiculously, I tried to find stars I knew. Breathing would have killed me if my all-purpose skinsuit, which was uber-smart, hadn't exchanged gases through my skin. The houseboat was also cutting edge. If asked, it could project a holographic star map, but that night I avoided talking with the computer and hearing its inhuman mimicry. I was tense, and reflected that an investment can be unsettling when it's your whole worth. Night, stars, sea, *bien*.

I closed my eyes and lay listening to the warm air. At last, I sat up scratching my depilated, enhanced scalp. The air spoke of water, night, and rock. And on top of that rock—thousands of miles of rock, the girth of a continent—only the vacant, soughing air. The ransom of my soul (I still called it one) would not buy, in this world, either the whisper of a grass-blade or the murmur of a single tree.

Dawn without birdsong.

Voluptuous was the day, and those that followed. I wasn't counting. (Who dared to count their blessings, these days? Or, not *these* days, but those chaotic ones I'd left behind on my one-way trip.) My Bath of Venus stretched an inexpressible shade of blue, like the essence of youth. I had what I'd bargained for, splashing off the deck into the transparencies, careful where I kicked. Creatures were everywhere, delicate and crayon-colored, and funny. The only man in the world chortled in his snorkel. Their innocence tickled me. The sea lilies were too exquisite to resist brushing their lace arms with my own. Floating, my shadow coasted over childlike sponges, and over streamlined trilobites zooming through the sandy bottom; it momentarily stained the pewter backs of proto-fish. They hadn't yet evolved jaws to eat others, but stuck to the sand, sucking on it. Goggle-eyed conodonts wove past like eels.

My toes hit sand, and I stood in a chest-high, gently waving sheet that bathed the land from (future) Michigan to (future) Mexico. Continental shield under my soles, sea in my arms, sky overhead, endlessness broken only by the houseboat that dogged me with its excellent tracking system. I looked around. What else was there to do? If I'd been a scientist . . . but I wasn't—nobody was really a scientist in the true sense anymore, it took large-scale public investment and all kinds of stability, social, economic, environmental, *tout*. Science, such as it was, served the whims of venture capital, and science had sent me back in time, because I'd paid, because it could. So much for science.

I made a friend.

It's possible that my friend was a departure from the norm, perhaps an evolutionary departure, but as a non-scientist I could hardly know. We met one morning. I liked the early hour when sea and sky were halves of a nacreous shell through which the eye of heaven peered, widening in discovery. After a sound sleep in the stateroom's rocking cradle, a shower in desalinated water, a shave, a dash of cologne—it was a beautiful morning. The task of jettisoning a (denatured) ball of night soil from the boat had become rather amusing, because my shit was a sensation with the proto-fish. The sinking ball boiled with their bodies, zigzagging madly. If their feast were an unnatural contaminant, well. They seemed quite happy.

I strolled on the foredeck, took coffee, and hummed a tune. Maybe, like my shit, my tune was a success because it was unique. Hundreds of millions of years before birdsong, it was the only tune in the world. As I hummed, a creature flew past the prow, plunged, and glided energetically alongside the boat. No birds, remember! No flying fish! The sea here was deeper, clear as glass. My escort was a whirl of topaz tentacles and rippling spotted mantle.

"*Bonjour*," I said, and tried humming again. The beast jetted out of the water, hung in the moist air, sparkling like jelly, long enough to radiate a sense of mission, and plunged back into its native element.

In this manner we passed several days. By night, he made himself invisible. I stayed aboard, endeavoring, first, to entertain my companion, and second, to capture him in videos and sketches. (Baffled by the creature's sex, I gave him a brotherly pronoun.) Lithe, nimble, very fast, he shone with intelligence and cheer that I failed to reproduce in images, no matter how detailed. But he was surely a cephalopod. That was unsurprising. I often saw groups of primitive squids, absurd creatures. They looked as if a coven of marine witches, in a fit of pique, had stuffed their many-legged familiars into the mouths of their pointed hats, which jerked haplessly through the water. My friend was different, shell-less like a modern cuttlefish, with slim, tawny legs, a spotted cape, and an elegant style. One day I slid, holding my breath, off the starboard side where he swam. To my joy, he darted over and we lay eye to eye. What an eye! A golden orb, across which pulsed a black slit shaped like a W, or a flowing wave. Indeed, it reminded me of a curtain tugged at the corners and in middle, concealing the dark chamber behind it, yet suggesting that revelation lay as close as a thought. We floated, equals in curiosity. Then we swam together, and though he left my side often, he was always back in the morning to jump for pleasure at the sound of my humming. I sang, too. What did I not sing during that bright time? Hip-hop, pop, nursery ditties. My God, for this pal of mine I sang "O Canada" in both languages, more or less.

What I didn't do was name him. I gave it much thought. One's instinct is to name a companion, if only with an endearment. There was never a being who better deserved the name of Felix. Yet the prospect of fastening to him a name, a human word, summoned outrageous vertigo, as if I'd been thrown into a bottomless well.

"Let's travel," I told my friend. "Let's go north." Although the Earth's continents were scrambled completely out of my bearings, most of them underwater at the South Pole, it was possible to sail to the future site of Chicago. I had no feelings for Chicago. But the magnificent corals that had thrived half a billion years before that city rose atop their remains, interested me. This was why I'd sold my auction house, enriched my attorneys, escaped my ex-wives, left my children, and bade adieu to all human folly on the failing planet. Simply to have this beautiful world to myself, with its ineffable corals. Corals!—in my time they'd bleached and died, the ghosts of our greed in the tomb of our seas. Humanity, the great despoiler, spoiled beauty. To cut my social ties was, for me, a religious act: penitential, ascetic, aspiring.

Once, long ago, I helped an Iranian couple unload a cargo of valuable carpets saved from the revolution. Head spinning with coffee and rosewater sweets, I was ushered into a store-room stacked with soft logs. Each carpet unrolled before my eyes sent a shock through my heart. By the time the treasures of woven art lay spread atop one another, indelible and epic, confessions of kingdoms, gardens of redemption, geometries of fiery prophecy—*enfin*, to make that couple rich, I vowed, was the least I could do. For myself, I bought only a small thing, very precious, which was not taken on the houseboat. What need? I had, here, what I'd bargained for.

On the day we arrived in Chicago, my good friend swimming alongside, I experienced that satisfying heartache a million times. Here were the carpets as I remembered them, but alive, swaying, burgeoning—for miles, in the teardrop containing the universe, I saw the flower of an immortal process that never slackened from primal intensity. The vision fulfilled my life. In other times, I had dived and hiked everywhere, had seen death in the glow of ice chasms and the night of benthic deserts; now, I was prepared to die in the Bath of Venus.

We stayed there a long time. It was necessary, when I wanted to swim without minding the coral reefs, to travel beyond them and take my exercise in open waters. During one such dip, I lost my friend. He was here; he was gone. I waited for many days and nights. I sang myself hoarse, I spat blood, waiting. In the end, I hoped he had found a mate and gone his way, that he hadn't died. He was a top predator, but no bigger than a spaniel; and this sea, *alors*, held man-sized scorpions bristling with armor.

I returned to Chicago, where the houseboat (it occurred to me for the first time) cast a shadow over a swathe of corals and their denizens: starfish, bobbing nautiluses, green and red algae, the usual customers. . . . For a Darwin, a Lamarck, a Joliot, the opportunity was infinite, but for me, well, I had not bargained for this usualness. No visionary solitude was here, just—the only place to be. In a word, Earth.

Without knowing my friend's natural lifespan, I could hope that, one day, he'd come back. I spent my time mulling over the videos and sketches that I'd made when he first came to the houseboat. Each recorded a wonder. None of them captured what I missed so much.

ANIMAL TRUTH

To the reader:
The rare fish, Metriaclima mowae, *known in Chewa as* mwamuna
woledzera, *and the genetic plague known as CMTX6, exist in the same
reality as that in which the Sphinx posed three fateful questions to the wandering Oedipus.*

PART 1

In her still sunny office, toward evening, a minor crisis awaited
the principal investigator of Mayhew Lab, who was already hard
hit and had hoped to collect her thoughts. Going through routine
emails, she hit an outlier. Jo Mayhew reread it, tapping a knuck-
le against her healthy front teeth. Then she retrieved several records—let no one say she'd suffered a "senior moment"—and
her memory matched the records.

The thing had to be handled now. It was a FOIA request.
Most of these were good faith uses of the Freedom of Information Act, but some were not; some were sneaky attempts to make
her lab share information before it was published. This new
request, however, did not fall into either category. It was much
creepier. She struck her keyboard as if summoning an extermi-
nator. Then she made a call on the speakerphone and talked her
contact through what she'd just sent over.

The request concerned a proposal by one of her post-docs,
Pradeep, for NIH funding. But whoever wrote the request didn't
give the proposal's correct title; no, they gave the title of an older version that included the word "evolution." Pradeep had cut
"evolution" from the title of his new proposal—the only one to

which the public had access. The older version could only have been seen by NIH personnel. Why, then, was Jo reading a FOIA request about the older version? How had the author of this request come by the proposal with "evolution" in the title?

Between Jo's pointed questions came the bubbling of her office aquarium, where her teaching fish swam. Behind her desk, in a blue slab of sky, two palm treetops rose above the windowsill. Stanford students who came to learn cichlid behaviors found themselves vaguely awed by those palm-tops guarding either side of the small woman, with a small gold cross at her throat, resting her arms before her like a sphinx. The students' feelings took the form of a cartoon taped to her office door, affectionately exaggerating Jo's full lips to resemble the cichlids'. Colleagues tended to speak lower in response to her surprising alto voice, which sometimes broke into a dark chuckle. Like the night sounds of a house, Jo's chuckle affected them depending on whether or not they trusted her.

"Mm," said her unruffled contact on the speakerphone. "A mole in NIH. Probably working for some gung-ho congressional staffer."

"That was my conjecture," Jo allowed, by way of venting. "Thanks."

"Oh no problem," chirped the other administrator. "We'll be in touch."

Jo was no stranger to political pressure, having worked for years in a federal agency, the NOAA. Coming on top of a worse crisis, though, this attack on her post-doc—on science—made her tip her chair back, shuck off her pumps, and flex her stockinged feet. She massaged her fingers against carpal tunnel and pressed tender points along each ashen eyebrow. Then lying back, a small upthrust jaw stretching the cords of her neck, she exhaled, like a smoker, the fatigue of shielding her lab from the continent-long jaws of anti-science politics. She'd been raised Republican. Her ninety-two year old father, whom she adored, still voted Republican, rain or shine. This persecution made no sense to her. What kind of leaders attacked American basic science? Jo woolgathered at these times, missing the world that had made her.

She'd grown up in New Hampshire. Her father, widowed shortly after her birth, had raised her; from his knees, she'd watched
the televised funeral cortege of President Kennedy. He'd taught
her to pray at bedtime when she was four, and the elements of
geometry when she was five. Of course, he'd had help in the
person of Mrs. Ida Bogan, his secretary. Mrs. Bogan's bulldog
countenance under a veiled hat, Mrs. Bogan's round shoulders
on which blouses zipped crookedly, had accompanied Jo to choir
practice and skating lessons. Mrs. Bogan had selected her ward-
robe and taught her basic cookery. She'd also guided Jo in the
question of heaven. Because if Jo's father, an engineer, meant
patriotic American science—the tallest skyscrapers and the cars
of the future on the longest highways and the atom bomb and
beating the Russians to the moon—Jo's mother meant something
less understood. On Sundays, visiting relatives would recall an
angel who had played tennis, sailed, and skied. *But you couldn't call
her a tomboy, she had the face of an angel, she's looking down from heaven
and is so proud of you*—a worrisome notion. An uncle's more satisfying picture: *Let me tell you, she could have skied professionally, I never
saw a woman take a jump like your mother, she'd hold that perfect V like she
was flying up to heaven.* This image haunted Jo whenever she was
brought, in starched skirts, to lay chrysanthemums on the granite
mirror of her mother's monument, which reflected clouds.

When she turned eight it occurred to her to ask a direct question:

"What was my mother really like?" Mrs. Bogan (who had just
lost her spouse to an afterlife as obscure as his retirement) replied,
*Your mother was like no other person I've ever known. It wasn't just what she
did, it was something about her. I believe there's a piece of music called Song
Without Words. That name reminds me of your mother.*

"Why did she die?"

No one ever named a disease. Her father would not speak of
what had been. Mrs. Bogan, making a fiddly face, spoke of *the
Lord* and *complications*, from which Jo gathered that her mother
was a superior saint. Unlike other saints, whose stories explained
their holiness, her mother caused awe without any story, just by

being herself, aloft on her skis. The idea of her mother gave her a breezy, free feeling, and that, she believed for the rest of her life, was the true sign of heaven. At twelve, for a confirmation gift, she was given her mother's small gold cross. *Your mother was wearing this when I met her*, said her father.

Jo never took it off. As she lay back musing, she fingered it in the slightly pulpy hollow of her throat.

Now she took communion as she did a long-distance run, on needful occasions, for if science was about discovering the universe, then faith was about staying focused on the big picture. Pride was the root of all sins: it meant forgetting your tiny part in the picture; and in Jo's book, trying to censor basic research was prideful. Of course, she knew why the public's ignorance served certain interests. She knew all that. She fought it. She needed a spiritual backstop, found it in the church, and dismissed ironies. All her life, she'd believed that an American mind had claim to science, and an American spirit to independence. Such were her values, though her political affiliation had changed in the predictable way for a career conservationist who was also female. She knew what had made her, loved it, and struggled to accept the mutations that time had brought. She would tell Papa when she saw him about the FOIA thing. He couldn't accept it any better than she could, though he'd lay the blame on different presidents. Yes, they'd have a nice debate. Then Jo would vote again for Obama, while Papa would go for Romney like a moth to the porch light.

Jo rubbed her lids gingerly, sat straight, and perused her bookshelves. Behind them, through the thin wall separating her office from the laboratory, she heard her lab manager, Ilya, droning some complaint. (He was an obsessive cyber-sleuth, a citizen of the digital world with murky professional antecedents, who'd made himself indispensable while incubating a start-up—and whom she had to chew out, again, tonight.) Covered in glass beads, a little hippopotamus twinkled on the middle shelf, ready to charge into the terrain of Jo's soul-searching. It was nothing less than that, she sensed. Within her groped a larval fear. The

crisis confronting her demanded a special order of attention. Not
Pradeep: she knew what to do there. This was about Leo, her
star post-doc, her collaborator, the young man into whose hands
she'd poured riches innumerable.

He had compared her to a monster. His words stung like
sea-urchin spines in her face—and Jo had had plenty hurled in
her face. This stuck. This raised weak, groping fear. It would be
necessary to stay late and try to think things through; she did not
want the problem following her home and spoiling her sleep.

She knew the monster. The monster was a key to her life. She
believed that she had vanquished it, if not gloriously like Saint
George, then effectively. Two years ago, Stanford had hired her
to replace a distinguished predecessor, Lewis Everett, after a very
hushed scandal. Everett was rich. His Los Altos Hills mansion
had a wing devoted to scientific antiquities where he entertained:
at his parties, it was said, caterers circulated with tiptoe caution
between vitrines displaying pearl-inlaid brass octants, first edi-
tions of Galileo, an Edison electric pen and other arcana. No one
questioned Everett's money until Leo became his post-doc.

Her first encounter with Leo had been—it struck her, now—
about the monster. Then, as the newly minted PI, she'd seen only
a blond boy who'd come by and dropped, crane legs and all, into
a chair. Sitting there shyly, he'd begun the sad tale of how Everett had forbidden him to publish the results of his experiment,
those results on which his best hopes hung. Listening, Jo noticed
the tapering eyes in his workaday face, the yellow irises, and his
accent—*the molecular mahdel, the bahdy.* Chicago? Ann Arbor, he
said. Grew up there, went to Michigan undergrad and grad. His
pale, fine hair shivered in its nimbus. Poor little boy blue. As he
leaned forward, his loose lab coat gave a glimpse of a lime T-shirt
with a beer logo. Humbly, he explained that he respected the PI's
authority, but he'd been forced to fight back. Jo reassured him
that such stories weren't unknown. Relieved, Leo spilled the rest
of it in his pleasant tenor. He'd been stunned by Everett's refusal
to let him publish, and terrified by Everett's threats. Not knowing
where to turn, he'd gone to Ilya.

"You know," Leo added apologetically, and she smiled. She'd taken her lab manager's rather sinister measure very quickly. In fact, what Leo and Ilya had done was bold. Armed with Power-Point and secrets (they'd even searched microfiche archives!) the two young men met quietly with officials from the same Stanford office that had copyrighted Google. There they revealed how Lewis Everett, through intimidation, had prevented his post-docs and graduate students from publishing. Over decades, he'd funneled their unpublished results to the tech start-ups on whose boards he served. *Ergo*, he'd gotten rich by stealing from Stanford. Soon after the meeting, Everett had resigned.

Her memory was in every sense tender; it hurt to recall how Leo had finished his story in a nervous pose, grabbing his side with one hand, and scratching his nape with the other. He'd just risked exposing himself as a whistle-blower to the new PI. But she'd liked him; she liked risk-takers. On the spot, she had released Leo from the project to which he'd been reassigned—a trivial project kept going as a sort of gulag for Everett's victims—and defunded the thing. That had been one of her most satisfying acts. No one could blame her for thinking the monster dead; at least, dealt with.

Really, what had she not done for Leo, her cruel accuser? She'd supported his research, as offbeat as his beer T-shirts. Gene therapy's cutting edge was CRISPR, but Leo was in love with bacterial vectors, so she let him synthesize genes and stick them in bacteria, filling a refrigerator with dubious strains. She'd introduced him to the rare cichlid, *M. mowae.* No one studied those fish, they were hell to breed, so—she'd urged—take a look. He did, and found a new gene. It was the gene she had predicted must exist: it caused a fatal hereditary disease in mowae, a disease she had discovered twenty years ago, in Africa. Hadn't her work, gladly shared, launched his?

Then she'd found the doctor whose deaf, half-paralyzed patients shared a flawed gene with mowae. This breakthrough had turned Leo's project into medical news, because if his gene therapy cured mowae, it could cure men. He'd become a rising star. And on top of everything, she'd recruited an angel VC. Hadn't she.

Sighing, Jo levered herself onto feet cooled by the tile floor. Ten steps south brought her to the window, the gesticulating palm tops, and the Life Science roofs congregated in the aqua blue of evening. She could hear buses wheeze on the avenue. Ten steps north, her lab coat hung on the door. A turn brought her opposite the wall-mounted aquarium and her teaching fish, the striped mbunas. Perpetually burbling water flavored the air. Jo stood fists on hips, and on the aquarium wall, a reflected woman drew closer, losing hips and fists, until a ghostly bust leaned toward the green water. Her hair slid in wings alongside the full lips; her eyes twitched, peering through their image to the fish hidden in green shade.

She'd done nothing wrong in the lab. She had to think through what had happened in London.

*   *   *

Jo returned to her seat, reached for her keyboard, and the office filled with insects' stridulations, frogs' creaking, and thunderous bursts of wingflaps. The live stream came from a wildlife reservation in South Africa. Jo liked having Africa at hand when she had to think hard. But she thought about London. Had London made her a monster? She and Leo had been standing by a window in the topmost chamber in Greg Kolayeff's guest townhouse, in Mayfair. The lights were out so they could see into the rain-beaten street.

By then, time had stretched and twisted until the night felt scarcely real. They'd flown to London in five hours from San Francisco, aboard the VC's private supersonic jet. They'd tried to focus on their iPads, while the planet dropped farther down the gravity well than they'd ever seen and the clouds turned to flaked eggshell. They'd caught each other staring at the wallpaper, and guessed it was Siamese croc. *We're flying*, Leo had said, *inside Greg's wallet*. After landing at City, they'd been rushed in a limo to Greg's offices, where the day passed in meetings with their VC and his panoply of consultants. Mayhew Lab intrigued Greg because he was afflicted with CMTX6, the degenerative nerve disease that Leo had cured in *M. mowae*. Too old for a cure himself, Greg cherished hope for his future sons (on the strength of which he'd married a Latvian supermodel). But if curing CMTX6 was a great thing, in Greg's book, the greater thing was development. Bacterial DNA could be engineered to make any substance, to treat the microbiome as well as genes—or as Greg put it, "Your bug that's a gene doctor can also be your bug that's a pharmacist." Leo had always seen more applications for his work than gene therapy alone, where CRISPR was dominant. He and Greg were a match.

Jo kept sneaking glances at Leo: she was proud of him. These were deep organizational waters, though not over her head. Greg had flown them here in order to make an impression, which meant that she had some leverage. Yet as the hours passed, the two scientists found that sorting out the details of excitingly useful plans from the details of wasteful, restrictive, or dodgy ones, while maintaining tact and aiming for compromise, was like hauling wheelbarrows full of gold bricks. Very inspiring it was, very grateful they were, and it wore them out. When Greg at last bundled them into his chauffeured Bentley, waving from his wheelchair like FDR, they'd ridden to Mayfair in the silence of travelers whose pained eardrums have not popped.

At the townhouse, Jo had bathed and put on yoga sweats; the guest suite's ivory interior arched its brows at her deshabille. Downstairs, she'd found Leo ferreting through a brushed-steel refrigerator. He wanted good old English stout, he complained loudly, but the only thing in here was this bullshit champagne. Jo wanted to drink it rather than go to a pub. She didn't feel like getting dressed again. (Had that been the first wrong step? Why didn't he go out alone? Had she prevented him?) Krug was James Bond's brand, Jo said. Consulting her iPhone, she announced that one bottle of the stuff cost the same as a new BioRad iCycler. They might as well try. After they drank, Leo suddenly wanted to look from the top floor window for Greg's garage, where the Bentley was kept. They'd drunk an iCycler and a half between them.

Upstairs, in the dark, by the cold window, between brocade drapes like folding doors, they'd reached a moment of stillness. They were high, not stupidly besotted. The champagne had made them in some way transparent to each other. Outside the street was quiet. Rain sounded like a chorus of sighs and sometimes like the clink of cooling embers. Leo couldn't see the garage, still they stood there and chatted, on and off, about the strangeness of their day, if what they'd just experienced could be called a day. To their relief, the carnival dazzle of their journey had faded, leaving pure wonderment. Jo's hand settled on Leo's upper arm. Yes, she had put her hand on him. She was to blame.

Yet nothing might have happened if he hadn't turned to hold her. She'd scoffed a little, told him to go out and find a girl his own age. He had raised his large hand to her face, and traced a circle on her lips. He had asked, *How would you even count the time we've been travelling together? Time doesn't matter, it's just us.* (Unsentimental though she was, Jo remembered his voice, with its endearing creak of feeling.) Then she had walked away. He'd followed. She'd come to him, still demurring. He'd promised to go away whenever she sent him. They'd kissed, and after each kiss, Leo had promised to go away whenever she sent him. Like two people giving a hand to each other as they climbed a stairway together, they had helped each other; it turned out to be one of those Escher stairways that seem to climb until they're revealed as descending, only to start climbing again.

Jo had never thought of sex as sin, but always felt at first contact with a man as her mother might have when her skis were airborne. Her lovers, for years, had been men of her own age; astute, grizzled friends in whose lovemaking she strayed not a jot from herself. With Leo, for the first time in years, she'd felt unsure. He had a way of holding her at arm's length, and at such moments under his gaze tugging at itself—as if he could not quite believe he was allowed to gaze, but found it very exciting—she knew that her small breasts drooped, and her thin muscularity was not an angel's. That shift out of herself required her to unmake, as it started to form, the memory of a mirror-paneled bedroom. Which unmade, she was herself again, under Leo's handling eyes that went before his hands.

She remembered the sweet shock of a young man's flesh, the grand crouching body all summer-haired, the cheek scraping back and forth against her inner thighs, like a creature scent-marking its range. He'd done nothing unexpected, and she'd enjoyed him completely. Once, she'd opened her eyes and looked past his heavy shoulder. From the porcelain bedside lamp, light washed upward, and at the fringe of it, a spot on the smooth wall seemed deformed. High on the cornice, a protruding mass. Gradually, she perceived that it was the cornice itself, ornamentally molded into a grape cluster; in her half-sleep she made out the plaster putti embracing the cluster, kicking their fat feet. She'd struggled suddenly and hauled up Leo's head by its silk roots to search the sleep-drunk face. She was seized by déjà vu: this wall, these thick sheets, this light, this face, and as the echo shimmered on and on, it vanished. Leo scarcely wakened and slid away. They'd settled back to back. And she had fallen into deep sleep, but now she remembered. A déjà vu.

*   *   *

Had she been egoistic, prideful? In judging herself, Jo faltered. Suppose she had behaved like a proper mentor, and sent Leo away for the night. Those hours. It seemed that life's hand had opened and those hours had sprung from it. Her instinct said that she'd been right to accept, that those hours had not made her a monster. Wouldn't sending him away have been spurning life, a kind of prideful rejection? Everything depended on the big picture, however, and on whether she'd betrayed her small part in it. But the big picture kept changing. That was the problem. That was the rub, as Papa would say. The whole episode might not have ruffled her conscience at all—she might not now be hanging around, wracking her brains like this, fear wriggling its eyeless head—if Leo hadn't changed. His change had turned her monstrous in his eyes, somehow. How?

Raw nostalgia gaped in her. He was her bright spot. Literally, at certain angles, Leo's hair outshone the laboratory glassware above his bench, a fuzzy sunspot as he opened a refrigerator and chose among his color-coded tubes of bacterial strains. Precisely because he was such a classic molecular biologist, more at home with data sets than animals, Jo liked to see him there, getting his hands wet. Once, on a local TV show, he'd enthused—*To me, synthesizing DNA is about transcending our evolutionary history.* In the weekly lab meeting that followed, he'd been roundly teased for public puffery. Jo had sniffed, *DNA is history. It's millions of years old and nobody invented it. What's to transcend?* He had laughed; he was sweet. The sweetness made itself felt. Now her bright spot was gone and she was a monster.

She turned to the watering hole in her monitor. The African night wore on in realtime; insects wove their song into a shining gray environment. Nyalas lay in the grass, turning their deerlike heads. It was quiet: crickets, faint whoops. A cough! or a bark? Quick as piano keys the nyalas turned this way, that way. One rose on her thin legs. Probably a dog, Jo thought. Her aquarium's purling and its mist scent seemed to rise from the water hole. Yes. She must think it through.

She checked her Apple watch, whose sand-pink band was a lucky accident: it matched her lipstick, encouraging her to feel that order might arise spontaneously. First things first. She had to chew out Ilya, who'd made trouble. It had started recently, during the usual crisis that beset all projects just before completion, a crisis so familiar in the lab that it was honored with superstitions: just as Leo's gene therapy seemed successful, his mowae had begun, all at once, to sicken. *Sick cichlids!* It wasn't funny. It was CMTX6.

Eventually, the problem was traced to the DNA primers, a routine ingredient that Leo bought custom-made from a colleague in Michigan. The primers were replaced, the project was saved, and Mayhew Lab breathed easier without the pong of dissected fish and the fear of a major failure. Then Ilya had cyber-snooped on the Michigan colleague, and turned up close ties to Lewis Everett. He'd told Jo, who chose to ignore the possible sabotage—if it was, which she doubted. Jo's way in dealing with monsters was to diminish them. But she had mishandled Ilya. Somehow he'd managed to irritate her unendurably, and she'd snapped, *Will you stop wasting my fucking time?!* The lab manager, affronted, had turned his sleety eyes and screen-reddened conjunctiva on her past.

He had unearthed certain records that she never discussed. Then he'd shared it all with Leo, his best friend; men *would* bond over perceived bitchery. Such was the price of losing her cool.

Now she rang up Ilya and heard him over the phone as well as through her wall, which conveyed certain truths the phone didn't always deliver.

"You shared my personal information with Leo," she said calmly, "without even asking, because you were pissed off. That was out of line. And very unhelpful."

"So . . . I want you to understand," Ilya hedged. "Nothing against you is in these files." Shamed y's slid into his speech. "They're in public archives anyyyone can vyiew, you know?" In the wall, muffled taps betrayed his booted foot's swinging. "So, am I fired or what?"

Jo waited. She rested her mind ten thousand miles away, among the nyalas who slept so lightly. Then she sighed. "Well, I need your advice. Are the fish rooms as secure as we can get them?"

Ilya replied in deep, loving tones that the area was under his close supervision and could not be more secure.

"Glad to hear it," Jo said, blithe and dry.

"So . . . how is Leo? Still crazy? He's sent me a lot of ridiculous messages."

"Leo's mental—stress is not your fault, Ilya, but the effect of sharing my information has been to damage his trust. Please take that to heart. He's like a capsized boat in fast water, it may take effort . . . to get him working again." They were supposed to be preparing for the Society for Neuroscience conference later in the month. A stream of experts would visit the fish rooms to view successfully treated mowae. Since the day that Leo had compared her to a monster, and walked out of the lab, Jo had been carrying his workload.

"Whatever you need me for——" Ilya was clipped, then contrite. "I feel not very good. I fucked up, okay, I am sorry, seriously! But Leo imagines security problems that are nonexistent. I am taking appropriate measures."

"Yes, let's check those," Jo agreed, adding grimly, "Thanks for your apology." She went over a checklist with him. Ilya's grasp of detail left nothing to be desired, and she felt better until he asked, husky with nosiness,

"Your shorebird research, you know the money it made in the diet industry? You could be lyiving like a queen."

"Mm. I don't approve of diet drugs." Through the wall came an incredulous neigh of laughter, and they rang off.

How did queens live? London's scents came back to her: stone, rain, plaster, heated wool, toast, potpourri, brine of love on thick crisp sheets. As for Leo. As for Leo . . .

Between her hands, her propped face sagged like a mask.

*   *   *

After returning from London, Leo had stopped coming to meetings at the lab as well as with the VC. She'd let it pass until Greg had invited them both to the Tesla factory in Fremont, to watch his new car roll off the line. His fun was their fun, of course, but Leo hadn't shown up. There had been uneasy jokes about forgetful geniuses. Jo had been furious. She dismissed the notion of Leo playing the spoiled lover, or ex-lover. Their night's adventure had been just that, leaving only a residue of warmth. In any case, Leo and slackness could not coexist. Something else was going on. She'd summoned him with an email from which the traces of her wrath had been carefully expunged. The approaching conference had her on edge, she realized; it was time to clear the air.

But when Leo arrived, she was taken aback. He usually wore a lab coat and Crocs for the damp-floored fish rooms. At lab get-to-gethers, he showed up in beer T-shirts, jeans, and dingy moccasins. For formal occasions, he owned a gray suit and dress shoes, which he hated. The first version of Leo was what she expected. He'd breeze in—white coat, drifting hair, clumpy Crocs—deliver his thoughts and breeze out. He should have come in like that.

Instead, he walked in and sat slowly. His T-shirt sagged; the moccasins bared his chalky hindfeet. His cheeks sank under their bone shelf. The hands resting on his thighs looked too wide-knuckled. Jo dismissed her reproaches, estimating that he'd lost fifteen pounds too fast. Resting her arms before her, grave and welcoming, she let him speak. But what he said made no sense. The memory of having disrobed before this troubled young man arose and struck her fleetingly as insane. She tried to choose objective phrases, tempered with warmth, that might restore the trust he ought to have. She hoped her care would make itself felt, and shut irony in the back of her mind, where it usually went.

"Leo, if you need to take a leave, be it medical or personal—and I don't have to know the details—" (She let that sink in.) "I'll help you. You get first author regardless. Health comes first." Leo's eyes turned the clear gold with which they viewed a poor result, and a shadowy Y showed on his forehead.

"That bad, huh."

"You looked rather frayed. We can record part of your presentation and play it at the conference. There are plenty of ways."

"You don't believe me." He'd turned away, a flicker at his heavy jaw's hinge.

Jo mustered her energies, lacing her fingers. "Let's review, so we're on the same page. A month ago, Ilya said that maybe Everett had sabotaged your project. We fixed the problem. Now you want to go after Everett legally, for scientific misconduct." (Leo nodded once, with vigor.) "Your reason is, you phoned him. You accused him of sabotage, and he denied it, and taunted you. You interpret his taunts as threats."

"Jo, he said our problems weren't over and he got really ugly."

"Those aren't threats—let me finish. Everett is a poker player. If he wanted to mess with you, he'd have been friendly. This is a wild goose chase. I need you to take a leave, or get back on your feet."

Jo's tones were measured but she knew her manner was full of snap, and when Leo climbed to his feet it seemed that he was taking her words literally. His hands hovered at belt height, recalling that there were no coat pockets to nestle in. Then one hand went over his head to scratch the broad nape, while the other hugged his ribs. He stood in the sixth-floor window's full morning light. It exposed a loose thread clinging to his sleeve, touched his glassy, working eyebrows, washed his flexed underarm with sun. He seemed to sway and creak, like a tree. Jo watched him with the vexed tenderness and detachment of age. It was too bad, the way the seat of his jeans bagged. She'd seen chimps take a pose like that, rocking slightly. He'd come out of it in a minute. The aquarium hiccupped, and Leo, hearing it, went to the tank and readjusted the filter. The water bubbled freshly on. The cichlids whirled and settled again.

"So, what do you say?" She sounded harsh to herself, but her star returned without fuss, crossing his ankles, and she had hope.

"I was adopted," Leo announced. "I haven't been forthright. I didn't accuse Everett of sabotage, I—we discussed something different. I apologize."

"For . . ." The PI rapidly shook her head as if clearing water from her ears. "Oh, for the meetings. Yes."

"Everett hates me because I'm his son." Leo regarded the stalled eyes, the frozen body across from him, and went on; the color returned to his sunken cheeks. Jo was monitoring her reactions: a stab of alarm, a flurried question of whether drugs or mental illness were here. She awaited a signal from her judgment. But if Leo had gone off the deep end, he was in lucid waters. This time, the story he told made sense.

It began when he was testing the bad primers. For controls, he had used the lab's human DNA samples. During the test, the computer had insisted that two of the DNA samples were identical, so one must be a duplicate; and it had shut down the program. Pressed for time, Leo had started over but skipped the second sample. Afterwards, he'd been curious about those two samples, because one was his own DNA. He'd racked it himself. So he had run SNPs on both. They weren't duplicates. No! One was Leo, and the other . . .

He'd never known his birth mother or his father. His adoptive parents had found him through a church charity, back in the day. The charity was long gone, as were most of its records, and he only knew that he came from overseas. (With this confession, Leo looked more himself; his expression convinced Jo that he was not delusional. He was only desperate, one of those who scramble over the sands of probability after a perfect dream.) The SNPs had shown Leo his, well, probably his father in an anonymous sample that only had a code number, right? So Leo had worked out—a way—to find the name of whosever DNA it was.

Jo's hand had risen to her throat, covering her gold cross.

"You do know that identifying human DNA, without the consent of the donor, is against standard research ethics." She paused, viscerally repulsed. "You violated ethics policy, and you used the university's resources to pursue your private interest."

"Can we skip the bureaucratese?" His voice was hard; she felt the chasm of experience between them, which, it was clear, he scarcely knew existed. He seemed on the verge of an outburst. Instead, he spoke with a sardonic mildness used to skewer people's errors. "I sent Everett the sequences and he agreed to talk on FaceTime. You're the only person who knows, by the way. I thought hard about what to say, right. I said—hey, we belong to each other, however you want that to be." Leo paused with no familiar muscle play in his face. Then he brought out his iPhone and offered it to Jo, who unwillingly took it. "Start from there. He's in the parking lot of the casino in San Jose. His choice," Leo breathed, "of venue."

Onscreen: night, neon parapets, and a face. Jo tapped the Play arrow. Lewis bent close, and beneath his split-bulge forehead and tufted brows, tiny agate cabochons peered at Jo. Leo's recorded voice was eager—*discuss the results, reach some understanding.* Shrinking, Lewis mumbled *fabrication.* He bobbed in and out of view unnervingly. *Why's that valet taking so long.* Teeth peeped under his mustache as Leo's voice rose. *Why would I fabricate something like that, why would anyone do that?* Jo saw the face suddenly as an object, doll-like, lolling inside the darkness of Leo's unanswered questions. *Because you're a fucking moron, and so's that pathetic bitch you work with.* Jo stopped the recording and handed back the iPhone.

Encouraged by Jo's silence, Leo proposed, once more, a lawsuit against Everett for scientific misconduct.

The PI had removed her hand from her throat, and spoke carefully.

"SNPs can be deceptive; also, you didn't have much coverage. I wouldn't jump to conclusions."

"You don't believe me." The gaze he turned on her was a sick boy's or an innocent old man's. A cup of coffee was at Jo's elbow, gone cold; she took one awful sip.

She began to discuss technical pitfalls to the testing Leo had done, not to prove Leo wrong but to turn him softly away from the Gorgon glare of his disappointment. Her words wound around him, and Leo's attention began to flag; he recrossed his ankles, knuckled the shadowy Y on his brow. Jo did not mention Everett: in the active geometries of her mind, a solid rectangle blocked out the former PI. She merely presented Leo with a plan. He would shelve his personal pursuits, since they were not time-sensitive, and return to his project, which was. He could take over in the fish rooms starting tomorrow, or the day after, if he needed to get up to speed. Which?

Jo gave her best smile. Everything curved upwards from her creaturely lips. Leo was moved, and irresolute. Life might have ups and downs, but the lab was the place to be: that was what Jo's smile had always meant.

"It's like—I tried to wrap up a loose end, right, only I made myself into a loose end. There's a loss of . . ." He broke off.

Jo reflected that Leo had had his share of betrayals. He'd fought to save his work from Everett's chicanery; he'd been dumped by a girlfriend (London had been a bit of rebound); and he'd had his project possibly sabotaged. Finally, this—weirdness—of his birth, and behind it, Jo sensed a primal separation that had always defined him. An image of rings widening on water rose to her mind; he wanted truth, the truth that made its movement darkly felt. Maybe it was no wonder he felt afraid.

"Well, Leo," Jo cut in cheerfully, "we've got a few hundred little boys in California who are at risk for CMTX6. Pretty soon, you can tell those kids' families that they won't necessarily go deaf or end up in wheelchairs. I'm looking forward to that. I think it's great. How about you?"

Her star leaned forward and cradled his face in his hands. Her heart was wrung.

"Yeah." He straightened, his face stained as it were by dry tears. "But, Jo. He's out there getting ready to blow my goddamn work apart. He's personally motivated. It's an issue we have to resolve, right?"

The PI had begun to feel terribly tired. Persistence was a great virtue, except when its possessor was achingly irrational and dead wrong.

"Everett is not about to disrupt my lab. I've been over this with Ilya, and it's a non-issue." Saying "issue," Jo grabbed a coffee-stained napkin, blew her nose, and scolded thickly, "You ought to trust me, you know? I've only been doing this for thirty years?" She turned to her computer and rattled the keyboard, mentally juggling schedules. "Okay, my dear, I'm giving you leave to go home to Michigan and visit your family." His parents: a beekeeping father, a mother who wore a *Frodo Lives!* button to city council meetings. Adopted or not, no unwholesomeness could be imagined there. There was nothing to his nonsense about Everett.

"You're throwing me out?" He was quizzical rather than angry.

"No, I need you back at work, but I'm giving you the option . . . as of . . . now. There. Sent. You'll let me know."

Dismissed, Leo didn't move while Jo went on with her work. Then his chair scraped. Footsteps shuffled, muted by the aquarium's tuneful bubbling. For his exit, Jo swiveled round with a friendly air of small tasks dispatched.

By now, the sun had risen higher, carrying away its presence and leaving the office in neutral daylight. Leo stood in this shrunken light, in the middle of the office. He had always stood in a fluid, irregular sort of way, as if rising through depths. Then, swiftly or deliberately, he'd perform some action that had been gathering momentum. Now he stood slack, holding himself together by the tilt of his head, with a look in the yellow eyes that jarred with his faintly stirring, spectral hair.

"I ought to trust you, right. Why didn't you tell me how Lewis stole your work? You never mentioned it. You never even mentioned you were his student. You never even shared that Ilya came to you with a warning—I had to hear it from Ilya."

Jo reached for her coffee cup, not lifting it. Instead, she held the base of the cup.

"Ilya showed me your paper. Fat metabolism in shorebirds." Leo tossed this out, to shift blame or unsettle her further. Between the two of them opened bottomless uncertainty. Walking to the door, he stooped to the handle, which until now he'd always caught mid-stride. Then he'd said—with that endearing creak in his voice—"I guess you and Lewis have a whole lot in common."

She remembered, after he'd left, turning the wrist that bore her Apple watch toward her, checking its face over and over without recalling what it meant. For nearly two weeks, she'd shoved the memory aside so she could work, while bits of it flared or faded. Only now had she reconstructed it as an ordered whole. Now it was her own humiliation that stole her breath. Remembering herself turned to plaster, clutching the stupid cup—when he'd said *what he had said*—and checking her watch like a broken doll, Jo felt doubled over with chagrin. She should have said something.

She got up stiffly and stood at the window. The evening sky was weightless stone, still too pale for stars. In the palm treetops, sparrows thrashed; and as the building emptied for dinnertime, the drone of low-temp freezers grew noticeable. From her feet, a sensation began flowing upward along her hamstrings until it took possession of her blood chemistry. She might break a sweat, the way it affected her right now: her nerves screamed to strike back, strike out, defend herself. *You and Lewis have a whole lot in common.* Outrageous. She should have said something. Leo was wrong.

His suspicions about her came from his own ignorance of professional ethics. The PI was under no obligation to dish dirt about the former PI. What did he think—that it would have been seemly to disparage her predecessor, to rake up old misdoings, in the ears of her subordinates? Leo was wrong, and she ought to be cool with that. The office phone rang: a student's long message irritated her until she lifted the receiver and slammed it down as if trying to make phone juice. She cursed aloud and didn't care if Ilya, behind the wall, pricked up his ears. This was why she'd never married. She took men into her life, and their assumptions tripled her stress. Do-it-all Jo! Jo the cheerleader, the picking brain, cook, therapist, maid! Ach. Good luck to you, boys. Glad to have been of service! She was trembling. She left the window.

No, that sad rant wasn't what she meant. Leo wasn't "men." Papa always said that when you're mad, figure out if the other guy has a point. Jo held her breath, then let it hiss away. Leo thought she had *a whole lot in common* with Everett. Outrageous. Never mind, did he have a point? On one score, just barely maybe, though Leo could know nothing of it. Yet he might know more than he knew. Unthinkable as it was, she must think it through.

*   *   *

On her monitor, trickling ink; it must be raining. Africa was no help. Slowly and with dread her mind approached the solid rectangle that blocked off the thought of Lewis Everett, and it became transparent. Through it, in darkness, the mirror-paneled bedroom; and in each of those tall panels a band of light; and in each band an agile, pale body whose bright hair tangled with another, duller body, repeated from all angles. She did not want to remember this. How attractive she'd been. She winced at the performance that was all tricks and capers, the spectacle that Lewis pursued sweatily and with bulging eyes fixed on his panelling. A spotlit bed? Even then it had struck her as stupid—though he'd been handsome enough, in rugged middle age, to attract a long line of anorexic Valley realtors. She'd been an outlier; graduate students weren't his specialty. To this day, she didn't know if he'd bedded her out of lust or research strategy.

To be sure, she'd been, not a beauty, but a hottie (as they said now) who had radiated self-confidence. She hadn't known it, except in the negative way of never fearing a refusal, but she'd put that down to men's availability. She'd spent no time on imagining how she appeared to others—in her jeans and rain gear and rattletrap VW, chasing sandpipers and curlews up and down the coast from San Diego to South Jetty. Everything she'd done then was like the joy of heading into a stiff wind. Now she knew the wind was time. Here she sat in Everett's stead, in a building that hadn't existed when she was his graduate student, in a part of campus that had been fields and live oaks, long before livecams, genomics, and NIH moles going after Charles Darwin. Was there an evil mirror, in those long gone days, that had caught not just her body's image but also her future, so that she ended up repeating her past with the seduction of a younger colleague?

Leo's words had a symmetry that seemed like truth. That was what fired her nerves with defensive rage. Truth, however, was her bailiwick. You began with the facts.

She'd known the facts so long, it took effort to see them anew. Lewis and she had played poker at a lab Christmas party, and she'd liked his laid-back style. When he'd made his move she was flattered, and in the few weeks it had lasted, between her trips into the field, she'd hidden her fundamental dislike of the situation (like an idiot) trying to pretend it was sophisticated. Sexual harassment it was not (she knew her Title IX). Yet what went on in the mirror-paneled bedroom had a foul, obliterating stupidity about it—a rudeness to her as God's creature, a rudeness toward the body—that was all the more distasteful for being unintentional, because Lewis (and maybe those realtors) thought he was a stud. He believed she was under his sexual spell, and she'd learned how difficult it was to sever intimate relations with your PI. (Oh, she should not have laid her hand on Leo!) She began to manufacture excuses, and stayed away until Lewis let her know that his recreation hours were "permanently booked." For years, Jo had wondered if the course of her career had sprung from her failure, at this news, to burst into tears. Instead she'd been respectful, sweet, and unable to hide her relief as she left his office. Shortly afterwards, he'd summoned her back and told her—as he'd told Leo, and many others—that her new work would not be published.

Jo had reacted like everyone else in that group of some dozen young scientists who, over the decades, had been gagged and robbed and believed themselves alone until Leo had shown otherwise. She'd run the gamut of incredulity, protest, and fear. Through it all, Lewis's poker face had stayed on, though his shaggy eyebrows had indulged in some pantomime. Her revulsion unbearable, she'd accepted almost instantly the need to change course and rid herself of an incubus. Despite Lewis's hints of retaliation should she complain, Jo, like Leo, had confided in best friends. She'd called her father (long distance, when that cost something) and told him all but the dirty parts. Supervisors who suppressed talent weren't news for an engineer, and Papa had been perfect as ever.

"Take my advice, Josie," he'd said. "Don't pick a fight with a skunk. Get going on a new track, and when you need help, let me know." Molly, an English zoologist from another lab, also heard the expurgated tale of Jo's troubles.

"Oh dear!"—*Eau d'yah!*—she'd exclaimed, alight with glee. For some time she'd been pressing Jo to join her at the research station, on Lake Malawi, where Molly studied a fish with the gloomy name of *Mormyrops*. There was easy grant money, Molly urged. Jo felt irked and toyed with. What sense would anyone make of it—since the PI had killed her work on shorebirds, she was going to take a crack at fish?

"You're done with shorebirds," Molly pronounced. "Through! Bollocks to Everett. He's a third-rater. Just put it about that you've contracted an allergy to birds, you know—feathers. You'll love the lake. You'll meet Ad Konings. Come on, you must." Molly was a beauty. Her rose gold hair and startling brown eyes, her height and graceful gait, were the stuff of sonnets. Most admirers failed to note that her small, soft, red lips were compressed, by habitual determination, into the shape of an equal sign. She was married to a UN official who worked part of the year in Lilongwe. In short, what Molly offered Jo, at that crisis in her life, seemed much more promising than anything else.

For a while, Jo's new life befell her like a lucky accident. She got the Malawi grant. Everyone believed her about the bird allergy. Lewis, finding her compliant, made no obstacles. Jo had never lied systematically before, and her lies' success was so unnerving that she travelled to San Francisco and made an anonymous confession in St. Patrick's Church, whose Latin mass Mrs. Bogan would have liked. She badly needed to make a clean breast of the whole affair, though she took the church's view of premarital sex with a grain of salt. Her confessor, urbane, and simpatico, cleared her of malicious intentions, mentioned the Magdalene, and with deadly aim asked her to think of her widowed father. She made her penance in the Yerba Buena garden, a green hilltop among skyscrapers buttressing the blue. Close to the sky, on a fine San Francisco day, she cherished the old, childish dream of her mother aloft in the smiling air. Absolution had restored her to her small part in the big picture, a girl who murmured prayers unnoticed. She returned home peacefully. A week later, she went to the clinic for a headache and discovered that she was pregnant.

Truly, she did not remember much about breaking the news. She'd been sleep-starved, barely able to drive. Lewis was a silhouette in front of a wincing window. She remembered that he'd chuckled and called her obscene names, silly insults, by way of denying his fatherhood. Partly, she'd been relieved: the prospect of his rising to embrace her with uxorious ardor had made her cringe. Partly, she'd drifted outside of herself and stood amazed

at the man. After all, it was his virility she attested to. With caution—Lewis could still damage her career—Jo offered him his
baby, no strings attached. She threw into her parched voice the
conviction that this was his baby, expecting the old poker hand
to know truth from a bluff. Again, he returned sneers, and Jo realized that his usual manner, which everyone called cool, was the
cold surface of an unfathomed hysteria. It was like outer space
chatter. Nodding off for an instant, she'd jerked awake with total
focus: she must know exactly where he stood.

She asked him what he wanted, what he wanted her to do.
Lewis cleared his throat and said something unremembered;
what still stuck was the phrase *saintly little girl parts*—a jeering mention of abortion, but in her woozy state she hardly knew what he
meant. Instead, a little girl had pinged into view, in starched skirts,
wearing a familiar face. Jo had left and gone home, gone to bed,
and told herself that when she woke, it would all be a mistake
or a miscarriage; neither came true, but she woke with a plan. It
was a half-assed, gonzo plan that had nearly killed her. Yet here
she was.

Jo sat in the dark. The rage that had possessed her was gone.
It was funny, how she hadn't felt angry about Everett in years and
years. When *had* she felt angry about him? When she'd staggered
out of his office on that day, over thirty years ago, she hadn't been
angry: she'd been stunned. But she'd found the next step; you
survived what was thrown at you by going the next step, and anger was a distraction. You minimized. You kept a certain cortical
cool. You dreamed of a glass cliff you tried to climb, that turned
into a bedsheet that wrapped around and floated you over the
ocean where you would fall, sink, and drown unmarked. Waking,
you scrubbed in the shower: good morning skin, good hips and
knees, good back and belly, good armpits, good strong legs. No
greeting for the growth in your flesh, for which you felt nothing so warm as hate; for which you felt nothing and even less.
Your soapy hands blessed yourself: the pregnancy you shut out of
mind. Wracked by nausea, you dealt with symptoms and ignored
the cause, as if you were having a spell of stomach flu. "No," you

told the doctor who administered your vaccines and Praziquantel (Lake Malawi swarmed with parasites) and asked per routine if you might be pregnant. You said it without thinking—No. Per routine you were not. Like playing cards, the idea of abortion flashed up in your mind right alongside the picture of a little girl-saint in starched skirts. There was time. You needed time. You packed. You weren't angry, you were busy. Instead of anger, crazy energy drove you all the way to Lake Malawi, and afterwards you'd had other things on your mind.

Your lost anger? For years you'd prided yourself on its absence. As an evolved trait, anger was a message of danger and a spur to action. But you couldn't have taken any action directly from your anger. No one would wish to hear your unsavory story about an established figure who'd done nothing illegal; your misfortune was no one's bailiwick; it fell into the realm of accident. It was like when a rock stubs your toe: that rock is not a reasonable target for anger. So you'd made Lewis Everett into a rock no higher than your toe, though he'd silenced your research and left his acidic semen to eat your future from inside you. You might have died, but took his job instead. Good girl. That's how you had thought of it all these years.

Well, and has your lost anger found you tonight, at last—across the years, through the slowly healed channels? Is your newfound anger the real reason you've become so outraged when a brilliant post-doc has a crisis, hardly an unheard-of event? Then you're not so angry with Leo after all. Your past is not his fault. No need to be angry with Leo. There, that feels better.

Jo groped in her desk drawer for napkins. The aquarium light was out, and her monitor had switched to sleep mode. The dark suited her. She really shouldn't take this evening off, with only two weeks till the conference deadline, plus having to carry Leo's workload as well—still, she must think things through. In the dark, so night owls wouldn't see her lights on and come knocking with their woes. Pradeep's best gel is irreproducible? Paolo left a mutagen uncapped? Sorry, the PI is not in right now. Jo clasped her hands behind her head and rocked her chair with one point-

ed toe. Weeping, she chuckled; how deliciously self-indulgent! So
many sopped napkins! Makeup be damned.

On her monitor, the rain had stopped; above the water hole
flew a rapid something that left white squiggles, likely a free-tailed
bat, cute as a button, no bigger than her hand. She wished she
could see it. She missed Africa. Funny how she loved the place
where she'd made her biggest mistake. Now was the time to think
it through at last; now that her whole being felt illuminated and
relaxed as if her callused heels shot light like flints, and her temples beamed. Now that her lost anger had come home.

Jo had often described the field station on Lake Malawi when
she taught her undergraduate seminar in evolutionary biology;
she'd tell them how it used to be in the eighties. The museum
had sent her there to collect, classify, and preserve cichlid spec-
imens and ship them back. Basically a nineteenth-century job:
take inventory. There were over 650 cichlid species in Lake Malawi; new ones were always turning up; this had been going for
a hundred and sixty million years, since cichlids became wide-
spread in the ancient landmass of Gondwana before it split into
our modern continents. In the African rift lakes, the cichlids
became isolated and begat strangeness upon strangeness. There
were cichlids that ate exclusively the eyes of other fish. Cichlids with enormous eyes saw one hundred meters down into the
abyss. Some played dead to fool their prey or built sandcastles
to attract mates. Gastronomically specialized cichlids ate only
snails; ate only crabs; ate only parasites off catfish; ate only bits
of catfish skin; ate only scales; ate only the eggs of other cichlids. There were males twelve times the weight of conspecific
females that lived in snail shells, safely away from their gargan-
tuan mates—though sometimes smaller males swam hopefully
into the females' shells. Adaptive radiation meant in practice
that the weirder the fish got, the weirder they were going to get.
You needed a sense of humor to be a biologist.

You also had to like living rough. The field station was a long
boxy place built not of the local baked mud but of real brick, yet
only the workroom and aquarium hall were roofed in tin. The

dorm rooms and kitchen were thatched. A generator kept the
aquariums running and lights on in the workroom; and an old
refrigerator gargled in the kitchen, so-called. The cook, Chisomo,
prepared the station's food outside on a clay stove, her famously
efficient *changu changu moto*. Meals were served on a trestle table
in the backyard, where gusts of woodsmoke flavored the *nsima*
porridge. Three closet-sized dorm rooms held two cots apiece,
swathed in mosquito netting, and were it not for the salubrious
green odor of thatch, the cots would have smelled. You bathed
in the lake; you relieved yourself hastily in the long drop, alert
for scorpions. Living rough, though, wasn't as much about the
physical conditions (not so different today) as the intellectual
conditions. There was no telephone service. To reach the world
beyond the lake, it was necessary to travel uncertain roads to a
distant town that boasted a telegraph or post office. There were
no computers. The workroom had two manual typewriters: a
Smith-Corona (everyone wanted that one) and a Hermes porta-
ble. But the greatest difference—the one that irredeemably sev-
ered past from present was the way you went about classifying
an animal. You had at your disposal your senses, hands, and basic measuring equipment. You observed the color, weight, body
shape, head shape, jaw size, and musculature in respect to conical
or tricuspid teeth, and so forth. Then you took your best guess,
because, to all intents and purposes, *there was no genomics*. Today,
any researcher could click on a site like Bouilla-Base and consult
databases replete with genomic information about cichlids. None
of that had existed when Jo had done the foundational studies of
M. mowae.

This far into the story, Jo's students didn't quite disbelieve
her, yet they couldn't quite believe either. Their clear young eyes
would be mistrustful. The dates they'd learned—Watson & Crick,
the Human Genome Project, and so on—did not match their
impression of the normal world being one in which DNA was the
key to life science. Jo might have been telling them about cutting
goose quill pens. Once, one of the bolder ones asked, "Didn't
paternity testing start in the eighties?"

Before she could reply, another student chimed in, "She's talking about genomics, not about, like, a couple of, like, totally low-throughput markers."

Smiling, Jo had steered the discussion toward the importance of observing animals first-hand in their habitats. But she'd been about to say, falsely, that paternity testing hadn't begun in the mid-eighties—because the thought of it had never occurred to her then. She'd been about to teach something false. The experience startled her as if her own younger self, the amateur liar, had manipulated her tongue. She'd dismissed the slip at the time, but now recollected it with an irritable gesture. Outside her windows, the night sky was deep into its hyperbolic approach to the true black it never achieved in the Valley. In Malawi, the sky was stuffed with stars. Let her remember. Yes, she remembered. Tonight, she could remember it all.

*   *   *

She arrived in the cool, windy season of July. She'd be at the beach cauled in sunrise, when the mountains were shadows. Whiffs of Chisomo's cookfire reached her, along with the lake's faint voices; fishermen were out there all night and into dawn. When her snorkel mask went on, she stopped smelling anything but vinyl. The first time she'd swum into the green-lit reaches, with their horizon of turquoise mist, she'd been expecting something like Hawaii. Instead, her visual sense went on overload. Her brain didn't work fast enough to sort patterns from the crowds, clouds and shoals of opalescent fish that swam past, over and under her, with flashing speed and wriggling movement, or hung their faces in hers like bug-eyed lamps whose skins crawled with colored lights. She remembered Molly's warning that the lake took some getting used to, and heeded her advice to float over a spot, just watching. Hours passed during which she drifted over algae-furred rocks; the floor was a giant carpet on which the outlines of sunbeams, falling through clear waters, wove an endless tangle. Overhead tumbled the sky of the fish, a silver meniscus in continual upheaval. She hung over her thin-legged shadow, absorbing information, waiting for the critical intellectual mass at which recognition would become instant.

Once, a burst of transparent fry wrapped her neck like a scarf, their tiny spines synchronized in terror of pursuers—and rounding Jo's neck as if it were a rock-shelf, the baby fish sped to their mother (who was hovering in circles) and into her open, working mouth. After which she circled a few more times, scooping up stragglers, a fry or two slipping from between her pewter lips like irrepressible remarks. Jo touched her neck. She'd seen mouth-breeders in aquariums, but now she'd felt the fry's panic, held her breath as they streamed to the safe mouth under their mother's lidless eyes. Jo had resigned herself to missing the operatic drama of avian life. As she learned to read the fish, however, they seemed sheer envelopes of emotion—mercurial with instinct, more powerful for their silence. When she broke her floating vigil to swim home, and batteries of brilliant creatures exploded from her stroking arms, she felt moved to be among them. Lake Malawi's cichlids were expected to be fascinating; she found that they were also good company.

How heavy she'd feel ashore, pulling off her flippers. As the mask dropped, in rushed the odors—exhalations of mountain woods, woodsmoke, sardines drying on racks, the lettuce-freshness of the water, diesel fumes from the speedboat belonging to Winton, the station's scuba guru and technician. Her mouth watered at the smell of Chisomo's cooking. How soft the sand was, walking to the station. Not even the whiff of formaldehyde as she passed the workroom's open doors suppressed her appetite; instead, it gave her a craving she tried desperately to ignore. Finally, she'd asked Chisomo for a cup of vinegar with salt. The young cook, elegant in her turquoise head-wrap and floral *chitenje*, looked at Jo slantwise across her high cheekbones. Softly, regretfully, she said that the vinegar had been put away and might take time to find. Jo confessed her ridiculous craving—"It's either that or drink the formaldehyde!" At which Chisomo broke into peals of dazzling laughter, accompanied by wise looks, trailing off in a long *heeeeh!*

Jo couldn't tell if the cook merely found her funny or guessed at more; in this country, she'd heard, pregnancy went unmentioned except to one's mother. Chisomo gave her a saucer of pickled wild figs, once a day. When Jo came for them, she found Chisomo's eyes meeting hers, and never knew what to say.

Jo's condition was sheltered by the lies she'd constructed. Before leaving Stanford, to prevent gossip in scientific circles, Jo had told Molly and her colleagues about an imaginary boyfriend: Charlie, a naval officer with a three-year posting in Okinawa. She'd driven alone to San Diego for the purpose of getting engaged during an imaginary farewell weekend; she'd baulked at buying herself a ring, but went hunting for secondhand men's shirts, which she liked anyway. For her father's benefit, she had cancelled her usual summer visit, saying that the vaccinations had made her weak. Her guilt was lessened by the idea of protecting her father. Papa was more sensitive than he let on; it would be impossible to hide her trouble all day, every day, for two weeks, whether or not he heard her retch at odd hours. She imagined presenting options to him. An illegitimate grandchild, by a man who'd hurt his daughter; an abortion, opposed by the church his family had served since the English Civil War; a child given up for adoption, bearing the genes of the angel-wife still mourned by every mirror in his pristine house. These considerations made Jo feel that her soul was being squeezed out of her temples in the shape of worms. She'd decided on an abortion, but in her own good time. First, she needed a new life.

For a few weeks, she had one. She'd never felt freer or happier than in those weeks at the lake. She might have flown back to the States on some trumped-up excuse, gone through her procedure, and returned truly free. Yet she delayed. Her new life claimed her; she fell asleep thinking of cichlids that swam in her dreams. Postponement became routine and she stopped looking at the calendar. The station's researchers came and went—zoologists, ecologists, evo-devo or fisheries people—making a social atmosphere that demanded little and rewarded focus. The rumor of Jo's engagement quelled the men's approaches to a swimsuited blonde, and for this neglect, for the sole time in her life, she felt grateful. The odd gleam of interest made her want to cover herself. Once, when she'd left the side of a very fetching Aussie who'd conversed for an hour through mouthfuls of banana fritters, his big square knees jogging for emphasis, the desire and repulsion churning together in her body made her clearly see an airline ticket.

The decision was within reach. She unearthed an appointment calendar from her suitcase, to force herself into setting a deadline, but the blank grid of days had the opposite effect. Her belly hardly showed. The nausea of her first trimester had lessened, and in spite of the facts, she didn't, deep down, really believe she'd had a "first trimester." She might have put on a few extra pounds from Chisomo's *nsima* with pumpkin-leaf sauce. What would she need to do? Find a ride to Lilongwe: there went a whole week in arrangements and the inevitable delays and snafus. Fly to New York, then on to San Francisco. Check with Stanford about her insurance. Rent a room in a hotel, and go through with it. She'd recover in the hotel room. No one would know. There would be gloved hands bearing steel, abdominal cramps, and afterwards a clammy secrecy that would linger forever. She promised herself to set a date soon.

Then she discovered *M. mowae.*

Her first contact happened at night, scuba diving, to observe the predator fish, *Mormyrops anguilloides*, which Molly called by their Malawian name, *chisembe*. Winton kept guard in the boat while Molly searched for the fish, Jo tagging along as an extra pair of spotter eyes. (It was on one of these searches that Winton had yanked hard on the line connecting Molly to the boat, and on surfacing they'd found themselves chased by an enraged hippo, a spouting mountain of murder, while Jo screamed with laughter like the idiot she was then. "Worst killer in Africa," Winton had said dryly.) The night lake was another world. Jo's lamp showed a shrunken field of drowned rocks, among which cichlids hid for the night. Gray chisembe glided by, with small, lobed fins and small, dour mouths; when they lunged, it was a few beats late. In the dark water, their hunting style was eerie to watch, as if the capture of each thrashing little cichlid (they ate only cichlids) occurred as an afterthought in a profound, morbid reverie.

Molly swam ahead, adjusting the mic boom and video camera attached to her with slow touches. The mic recorded a weak electric field surrounding each chisembe, made by an organ in its tail and monitored by its electro-sensitive skin. When prey swam near, their forms interrupted the field, casting a sort of electric shadow over the predator. That was why chisembe seemed so disengaged, until, having felt a fish-shaped shadow pass, they were moved to attack. On that particular night, Jo was enjoying herself; the chisembe had (as she and Molly used to joke) a special magnetism.

She swam in loops parallel to Molly, following up on the recorded fish for anything noteworthy. Beneath her headlamp, a chisembe was hanging out beside a rockpile. A sudden flash below her made Jo snatch at the water, then at her gold cross— she'd been certain it had dropped from her. Relieved, she stared down and saw a long, shining fin twisting in the wake of a small dark cichlid that acted in a way she'd never seen before. To her lower left, the cichlid, with its shining fin, started to swim away but dropped headfirst, plummeting a few inches; the small body yawed and struggled to right itself, while its fin by no means waved erect but billowed and wrapped awkwardly. Then the small fish tried to rise, nose first, and beat the water pitifully before drifting onto its side. Meanwhile, almost under her nose, the chisembe poked along in its electric vigil, fluttering its oyster mushroom fins, and swam into the small cichlid's area. Below the cichlid, the rocks held safety, so near that Jo could have stretched out her foot and toed them. Anticipating, she sank lower, but no small gaudy fish darted to shelter. Instead, the drama played above her, in her headlamp's funnel beam, bubbles streaming past.

The cichlid tumbled in its golden shroud; it wriggled free and abruptly swam a little way, enough for Jo to suspect it was a parent fish feigning injury to distract a predator from its offspring. Such feints typically ended in quick escapes. The chisembe swam nearer to the small fish, which thrashed about and, again, plum-

meted—this time, right past the chisembe, casting a fateful shadow on its flank. Without delay, a cocoon of sorts jumped about in
the chisembe's hooked jaws as it swam off trailing a golden shred.
No escape, then. Jo peered and poked about the rockpile, search-
ing for clues, until she became aware of loud bursts of Gurglish,
the nickname she and Molly had for yelling underwater. On her
periphery, in an oval of rayed light, Molly dangled with the mic
boom and camera hanging off her like cherubic attendants on
the Ghost of Christmas Scuba. Jo hurried to swim alongside her.

Later, they clambered back into the speedboat and shared a
thermos of tea. The starlit lake looked too smooth to be water;
far off, a dugout canoe dispelled the illusion, gliding on a black
thread. Winton steered slowly, a bottle of Carlsberg in one hand.
In the night sky, stellar traffic was so congested and bright that
his bottle was tinged green. Molly talked about the dive, mainly
to Winton. A compact man in his thirties, he'd been a guide at a
nearby vacation resort, but had quit because he couldn't whistle
fish eagles out of the sky. Everyone wanted a guide who could
whistle for a fish eagle. "I'm the only Black man who can't whistle," Winton would explain, waxing ironic, when asked about his
former job. He was happier at the field station, where he ran the
boat and a troop of assistants, and shared with scientists the lore
of the lake that infinitely interested him. Molly knew none of her
words were wasted on his stocky back.

"I saw a chisembe stun a cichlid," Jo ventured. "I think—it
stunned it."

"What on earth do you mean, 'stun'?" Molly fluted, toweling
her hair. "Their charge is quite weak." Jo described the cichlid's
struggle. The wind of their speed raised bracing shivers that they
allowed on their skin without troubling to cover up. They'd just
agreed that the cichlid might have been ailing in some neurological way, when Winton cut the throttle and turned towards them.
When he smiled, his thin mustache, from nose to chin, circled
the curve of his teeth. The effect was like watching ripples widen.

"This fish," he said, "Its name is *mwamuna woledzera*. Yah!" He
broke out laughing with Molly, whose wrists drooped over her

slim knees, a wet lock painting her cheek. Conversation in Chewa added to her irritating perfections.

"It means *drunken husband*," she translated.

"Says it all," Jo replied. "Funny. I wonder if only the males swim like that?" Both scientists looked at Winton.

"I don't see any females swim like that," he offered. "I don't know, however. This is a fish of no value—throwaway catch. It has a disease of some variety." He turned back to the wheel, guzzled, and started them again along their starlit course.

For too long, the grip of hunch had been absent from Jo's life. Rejoicing in it, she combed the station's library and found that her fish had been observed in 1899, and named *M. mowae*. M for *Metriaclima*, genus of Lake Malawi's haplochromine cichlids; *mowae* from the Chewa for beer. *Mwamuna woledzera* appeared in a quaint translation, without comment. Truly, no one else had been interested in this fish. She set herself to investigate. Winton's crew built weirs and ran nets wherever Jo's fish were spotted. Paid by the catch, they complained that the species was as rare as it was useless. Jo and Winton raised their pay. By late August, her wild stock were well established in their tank. She nicknamed them 'the *mwamunas*,' which was ungrammatical, as Molly didn't fail to point out, and rather sexist toward the females.

The workroom had sunlight by day, and stark festooned bulbs at night; during the day, its tall doors opened onto the beach. At night, for fear of wild animals, they were shut. Long rows of aquarium tanks stood parallel to one another all the way to the end of the hall, where a sump sink gurgled and swished. At the other end, a raised alcove held a desk, reference books, a pair of microscopes with basic accoutrements, and the typewriters. Sitting above the moist babbling hall, Jo sometimes felt she was in a cockpit, flying blind. At night, the hall's windows endured a pattering assault of moths. A tin-framed photograph of Hastings Banda, Malawi's president for life, looked over her activities with the expression of a famous doctor whom a patient has ventured to question.

Jo had a hunch that the drunkard's walk, or swim, of the *mwa-munas* was an inherited neurological problem. Heredity could only be established by breeding the fish and observing the new generations; meanwhile, she experimented to see if the trait were caused by infection from bacteria, fungi, or parasites. Through the logic of isolations, combinations, cultures and tests, the drunken husbands produced negative results for infection. These results supported her hunch; she could call it an hypothesis and proceed.

Instead of arranging for a ride to Lilongwe and thence to San Francisco, for her abortion, Jo embarked on the task of breeding true.

September waned, and the weather warmed. Molly and Jo spread towels on the beach and enjoyed sunsets together with the other four stationers as they came and went on shorter grants. Molly would insist that they oughtn't to call it a sundowner as there was no touristy gin, nothing offensively colonial; still, the sunset watchers were usually white. Malawian, Zambian, Kenyan colleagues went drinking in the village where the *chibuku-mama* served her fresh brew. The rest sprawled on beach towels in a warm breeze, watching a molten strip on the horizon mass into a fireball, and the deep blue lake, 300 miles long, become a smooth body on whose surface the hues of all its denizens seemed dissolved, from burnt red to cloud blue, like a planet-sized cichlid fanning its fins in endless ripples along the darkening strand. In the dusk, under a lemon sky barred with clouds, they passed around what looked like milk cartons, sucked at fermented maize, and smacked their lips. Jo wouldn't drink because she didn't like beer, and *chibuku* was a beer that crunched in your teeth.

"A drop won't do you or Junior any harm," said Alex, the big-kneed Australian, in her ear. She could feel his warm breath. Her face seemed to fall open, and Molly, kicking a pointed foot, said,

"Alex, shut up. Oaf."

"Oaf?" Alex's feelings were hurt. "All right then." He rolled to the other side of his towel and contemplated the view. In the amber sky, on high rocks, perched the silhouettes of cormorants. Jo hugged her T-shirt, knotted to conceal the bulge; her jeans were a little tight. Not "junior" tight.

She went to bed early and lay on the hard cot whose sourness edged the cured-green scent of thatch. Molly came in and undressed, the discreet beam of her flashlight crosshatched with mosquito netting. She lay down and whispered Jo's name. It wasn't unusual for them to talk at night, and when Jo answered, Molly—who didn't want to pry—asked when she planned to return to the States, or would it be Okinawa? Into the darkness erupted the wood-chipper chatter of vervets; a hawk must have gone over the mango tree. Then all was dead quiet except for the insects.

"Soon, I guess. There's so much new work. I hate to leave."

"If Charlie knows . . ." Molly paused. "He'll surely want you out of Malawi and under the best of care." Jo said nothing. "It's not my place, I know. But you can come back. Your drunken hubbies will wait." Jo didn't laugh. "I'll drive you to Lilongwe myself, in the jeep, when you're ready?"

Jo had never heard her friend so gentle. She thanked Molly, and pretended sleep, while the shock of her fate rang and rang. From someone managing a private disorder, she'd become something public: an *expectant mother.* Not only did the idea not describe the knot in her belly, it deeply wronged her; it opposed her intent, it falsified her very breathing. Bolts shot into place on all the lies she'd told to free herself; she was now their prisoner.

*   *   *

Day by day, in their isolation tanks, the *mwamunas* revealed to her a progressive disorder that went from bad to worse, yet did not kill the fish outright. Instead, it wore them out. They could not keep an even keel in the water. They yawed, pitched, spun like waterlogged tops, and drifted to the bottom, where they lipped at the gravel or lay still and died. Examination showed that their ventral fins became increasingly swollen. Dead *mwamunas'* fins were like little balloons, due to inflammation. One afternoon, when Jo had graphed her measurements of ventral fins, and saw the curve of their inflammation against time, she raised her eyes to the portrait of Hastings Banda without seeing him and slammed her fist on the desk in triumph. The problem had looked neurological to her from the getgo, and a nerve disease could cause this kind of damage, couldn't it? *Yes.* But she had so little information. Like cichlids flickering into underwater view, questions swarmed around her new data. Why were only the mature males affected, why not the juvenile males? Were the females really immune? What percentage of the population was affected? When and how did the disorder start? What about environmental factors? In short, she had no baseline. To get it, she had to breed a few generations.

She had already begun. She had two breeding tanks that held a single, healthy male and several females; and she'd prepared special tanks for females who were "holding," brooding fertilized eggs in their mouths. She also knew why the *mwamunas* had not attracted more researchers. Drunken hubbies! Males in the breeding tanks got sick—a healthy male, at breakfast, was swimming "drunk" by suppertime—and she had to start over with a fresh one from the wild stock tank. Males in the wild stock tank got sick, and the assistants, politely cynical, were sent to get new males. The new males, introduced into the wild stock tank, fell in frenzies on one another and ripped and rammed and bled. Then the wild females, put into the breeding tank, expressed their social stress by spitting out fertilized eggs before Jo could get them to their peaceful "holding" tank. *Fuck motherhood in this crazy world!* spat the stressed females. Jo took the point but grimly persevered. She had the discipline to envision her desired end: the "holding" tanks filled with mothers and their circling fry, her own lines of true-bred *mwamunas*, and her questions answered. Inevitably, she wished she could spit out the knot in her belly.

Never again would her mind be so strange. At work, she was filled with joy. You might have shaken her and stars would have fallen out. But when she sat at the trestle table among her colleagues, all fondly deferential to an *expectant mother*, she was a nerveless clod. Between what had to be done, and what she felt able to do, rose a prodigious yet indecipherable shadow. "Pre-partum depression," they'd call it now; a fancy name for what happened to a woman whose pregnancy stole her will.

"What does your Charlie look like?" Molly called to her across the table. With a tin fork, Jo was pressing tracks into her sticky *kondowole*, warding off nausea. Heads turned; the free people of the world, whose bellies held only themselves, waited for her to meet their sticky expectations. "Have you a photograph?" Two bee-eaters plunged between Jo and the others, divine mercy—their fluffy orange heads and green boomeranging rumps distracted everyone but Molly, who, however, desisted.

Summer arrived in December. Thunderheads climbed with terrifying swiftness to the top of the grey sky and their crashing made everything else inaudible. Fireflies floated in the bush. Jo had entered her third term. In the vanished time—time she'd let slip through her hands as she pursued her work—her own body had become a hostile power. Her bed was a sweltering shelf. Her gut roiled and eructed at both ends over so much as a spoonful of food, yet she was plagued with unsatisfied hunger. Hands, feet, arms and legs swelled, itched, and dragged. Her back alarmed her with popping sounds and stabbing pains. Her breasts, once small, overflowed her hands when she examined the aureoles of her sore nipples, spreading like bruises. Her body got in the way when she needed to scratch mosquito bites. She suffered from constipation, and endured stinking vigils in the long drop, afraid of scorpions; and these vigils were repeated, weirdly embellished, in her sickening dreams. All this, she pitted herself against as if it were a headwind. She bent into the wind and took one step after the next. No abortion would happen now, she knew; she was going to bear a child; what would happen afterwards concerned her less than that the pregnancy would end. When it ended, and the baby began, the baby would be the size of Lake Malawi and she'd swim or drown in the situation. She'd take it home and adopt it out somehow, solutions would suggest themselves. Until then, with unthinking ferocity, she refused to abandon, she cleaved to, her work with *M. mowae.*

Yet a precious balance visited her body at dawn, walking on the sand, the peacock glitter of the water emerging from night. She'd hear Chisomo singing to raise her spirits, as she lit the fire in her stove. Then Jo's sense of degradation eased, and it seemed as if another voice were shouting from far off, over a high wind, words she couldn't hear yet whose import struck her heart. She must run for her life. She must take her belly on a plane, go, and make arrangements. She would stand still and listen, until the indecipherable shadow rose again between her and the voice of salvation. Then she was left only with blind resistance to letting Lewis Everett stop her work. Besides—besides, she told herself, cherishing the thought—she was on the track of something remarkable.

Not one of her male *mwamunas* stayed healthy. So far, every one of them succumbed to the drunkard's walk. Many reasons could account for this, but the guesswork would soon be over. Her captivity-bred *mwamunas*, she saw, matured faster than normal for cichlids. Much faster! Both males and females raced toward adulthood, and especially surprising were the egg spots. Egg-shaped spots, on the fins of male *Metriaclima*, induced the females to open their mouths, thinking they'd left some eggs out—at which the males sprayed them with milt, fertilizing all the eggs in the females' mouths. Egg-spotted young *mwamunas* were a bit like eight-year-old baritones. Jo began to posit a species that only just clung to viability by speeding up maturation, in order to reproduce before the fragile males died. They grew up fast because they wouldn't be here long, perhaps. She would find out, she promised herself, whatever it took. This was her discovery.

Never again was her mind so strange. Remembering it was like watching a foreign film without subtitles; the action was clear, the meaning elusive. As an explanation, "pre-partum depression" didn't go far. Molly, though, had understood. Molly, who had grandchildren now, lived in Sussex, punctually sent Christmas cards, and kept Jo on the roster of benefactors of a village school beside Lake Malawi. Molly who had saved her life, after humiliating her so badly.

She remembered it was a bright hot day. She was going to the village, to buy the patterned cotton wraps that Malawian women wore, since her drawstring pants were threadbare. Molly was driving the station's vintage jeep that had been fun, once, but now felt like sitting in a blender. Molly tried to make her talk. For weeks, Molly had been dangling hints from which Jo inferred her friend's evolving ideas. Charlie and Jo might have split, since he never wrote or telegraphed. Or, Jo might be keeping her pregnancy secret from Charlie. Of course, Molly's intentions were excruciatingly good.

Maybe because the jeep jolted it out of her, Jo said outright that she would have the baby in Africa. For a bumpy mile, she listened to Molly develop an impromptu plan to send her to Johannesburg, where Molly had cousins and the hospital was decent. Jo thanked her but said that she wasn't going. She would give birth by the lake.

Molly was incredulous.

"Why not?" Jo asked. "The village women do it all the time."

The jeep slowed, churned to the edge of the road, and halted. Under her boonie hat, Molly looked pale about the lips, which were flattened in an equal sign.

"This would be your stop?" she chirped. "On your way now." And when Jo, baffled, didn't move—"Not keen to walk in the mud?" Crystallized anger pinged off her consonants. "Chisomo does it when she can't get a lift. Why not? The village women do it all the time. They don't own cars."

"I didn't mean it that way," Jo said limply.

With vicious acceleration, Molly got them on the road again. "Oh, but I think you did mean it that way," she cooed. "Unless you know the rate of maternal death here? I thought not. Twenty-two percent of Malawian women die that way. Chisomo's mother did, you know. That's why she cooks for us, instead of attending school. She has three little sisters to fend for. "

"I'm sorry," Jo said.

"Ohh," Molly groaned. "Sheena, Queen of the Jungle, says she's *sorry*."

The rest of the trip did not even leave a memory of buying Jo's *chitenje*. All Jo would remember was how she went back alone to the stuffy thatched room and lay there, ignoring work and meals and the effort of thinking, until she lost track of time. In the darkness she heard Molly whispering.

Jo opened her mouth, and no words came. Molly's flashlight stroked through the mosquito netting.

"Are you all right, Jo?" Closing her eyes, she felt Molly touch her forehead, checking for fever.

At the officiousness of this, Jo rasped, "Charlie doesn't exist. I don't have a boyfriend. This is my mess, and I'll thank you to stay the hell out of it." There was no reply, and Jo felt she'd fallen into a pit. Some time later, a cool surface brushed her cheek, and she found herself drinking cups of water, sitting up eagerly for them.

"I've been a bear," Molly said. "But I do mean to help. I brought you here and it's my job to get you home safely."

"It's my job," Jo sighed. Afar off, in a lake of insect song, the plaint of a fisherman could be faintly heard. The air in the room was still. Each breath was like warm salad.

"Was it—the pregnancy—"

"I wasn't raped. I had bad judgment."

"Ah. And you're using the pregnancy to punish yourself. That seems very clear."

"No," Jo objected weakly. "I just procrastinated." (She remembered saying this—it wasn't that she'd ever forgotten, but she'd never paid attention, and as she did, her words seemed those of a girl in a play.)

The discoverer of *M. mowae*'s inherited disorder found her life more bearable after this confession. She'd lied for so long that she'd forgotten what a burden it was to carry walls around herself. Although Molly kept her story secret, (and, tactfully, never asked her to name "the guy,") Jo felt friendlier toward everyone. In return for pickled figs, she made a gift of her spare slide rule to Chisomo's sister, a schoolgirl whose cropped head was the same shape as the cook's, borne more lightly. Family resemblance was no longer a painful topic; her horror of the pregnancy diminished. She'd find out what the big deal was about childbirth, she told herself.

Over Christmas, Molly left to spend a week with her husband in Lilongwe, promising Jo that she'd "sort matters out." Jo, admitting she had no idea what to do, spent Christmas alone, relieved not to have to think about anything except a certain blunt-faced, egg-spotted, mysterious fish that swam again in her dreams, now that their current ran clearer. Observation, measurement, damage control, and maintenance occupied the peaceful days whose rains brought out all the green in the woods, and all the birdsong in the trees around the tranquil lake.

Molly returned, softer by a few pounds, rosier, and optimistic about her plan for Jo, which she'd cobbled together with the help of her husband, Ian, and his embassy contacts. She'd found a private clinic run by an expat Austrian doctor who was highly thought of, discreet, and able to deliver a baby. The clinic was, by the standards of Lilongwe, well equipped and staffed. Everyone spoke English. The best part (which Molly called the pièce de résistance) was that Dr. Baeder worked with an evangelical charity that ran an adoption agency; they placed illegitimate Malawian children in rich world families. Jo must come and stay in Lilongwe. They must leave as soon as possible. Anything might happen to the roads, or to Jo herself, if they delayed.

"Who's going to take care of my *mwamunas*?" Jo fussed, and went to look for Winton. Days, a week, and more time passed as she labored to create routines that the assistants could follow. She felt she would never be satisfied that the wild stock, the true breeds, the mothers and fry, the holding females, the sick males and the healthy, would be cared for and documented adequately during her absence. She made baseline notes on the condition of each tank, physically, socially, and with regard to individual fishes' health, behavior, age, and needs. She begged the assistants to follow her directions to the letter—their gentle promises proved only that Malawians said what pleased as a matter of courtesy. She begged Winton to keep tabs on the assistants, which he said he always did, not looking at her, and laughing uncomfortably as she resorted to her miniscule Chewa and mispronounced *chonde*, *zikomo*, and again *chonde*, on notes of rising anxiety. Chisomo, who'd begun serving Jo a cup of baobab juice at breakfast, took the unusual step of explaining, in halting English, that the baobab bark, put in bathwater, made babies fat and strong. And she smiled, slightly to Jo's side, with warmth. *Zikomo*, Jo said. Chisomo forbore to correct her pronunciation; Molly, however, did not.

Day after day, Molly waited and (she confided later) worried. She worried through sundowners on the damp, squeaky beach, when lightning flickered like flashbulbs. At night the sound of waterfalls could be heard through their pillows. Molly foresaw bridges washed away, roads closed, Jo entering labor scandalously in some muddy hole. One clear and windless morning, she resolved to get on the road by means fair or foul, but nature spared her the effort.

Jo stood on the beach shouting with wonder. Molly joined her. All else was forgotten. Growing vaster by the second, a smoke plume towered from the broad blue lake, where there was nothing but water, into the vault of the sky. Jo was seeing it for the first time, though she knew what it meant. Lake Malawi was half a mile deep. On its bottom crawled the larvae of mayflies; once a year, they cocooned themselves, floated multitudinously to the surface, hatched all at once, flew into the air—exactly resembling smoke—mated, and died as their fertile eggs sank toward the abyssal floor. *Ephemeroptera*, things of a day whose cycle endured like the stars. All time rose up before the friends' eyes; all time reproduced itself and fell back to its origin. It looked like a fire and it was life.

Then, Molly said what neither of them could ever remember, exactly, but they left without further delay.

*   *   *

Molly and Ian lived in a bungalow belonging to the British embassy in Lilongwe, where Ian did something Jo had since forgotten. She recalled resting on the verandah, in a deep chair of creaking cane, near the cool brick wall. The tin roof's shadow fanned over the floor, down the steps, and into the garden as the day wore on. Swarms of orange and pink bougainvillea wrapped the front gate. Ian, a brisk yet mild man who treated all humanity as people he'd met somewhere before, would come from the office at four o'clock and stay for tea. Jo's sole duty to her hosts lay in praising their teas, brought from home. The tea steam dissipated slowly, perfuming the verandah until rainshowers swept down and spread the musk of tomato vines and ripening maize. When Molly wasn't busy, she and Jo spent long hours catching up on the literature; an orgy of paging through neglected issues of *Cybium, Journal of Ichthyology, Journal of Tropical Zoology, Animal Behavior,* et. al. Jo remembered a cover of *Time*—Steve Jobs!—and how she'd searched in vain for pages sliced from the magazine. The phone was tapped, her hosts offhandedly told her, and their mail opened. Politics were never discussed around the gardener, his gofer nephew, or his wife, a glowingly proficient housemaid whose greeting was, "You are welcomed."

These three Malawians struck Jo differently from those she had known at the lake. They seemed somehow bulkier or physically nearer than Winton, Chisomo and the villagers, as if the clear medium of reality had a different density here. She noticed things about them. Like how the middle-aged gardener, leaning on his hoe, habitually touched his right trouser pocket where something of value kept its place. How the teenage nephew, leaving by the gate, took with both hands a basket of home-cooked *mbatata* from his aunt, whose expectations of the boy straightened her shoulders as he went.

Once, when Jo stood heavily in a doorway, unsure where to put herself, the housemaid tilted her graying square-browed head and said pleasantly, "Feel free, madam. Feel free here." The Chewa-speaker's way with r's and l's made her words sound almost like, "Fear flee." It hit Jo that she was in a country not her own. For days, she mulled over this absurdly belated discovery, this obvious truth, and what it could mean. She remembered Molly's anger on their drive to the village, when Jo had trotted out her lakeside birth fantasy. That was it, Jo thought. Molly had shocked her out of lying—about herself, about others. That shock had changed her. Now, Malawi and its people were no longer an exotic backdrop for studying cichlids. There was no backdrop. Instead, there was something like the very fine net that fishermen rowed out to submerge, yard by yard, in the lake, to catch the tiny fish called *usipa*. Inside this billowing yet confining net, suspended with the house staff, Jo felt subtle tugs of tension and accommodation, cordiality and reserve. Her heart was caught and somehow tutored to understand that although the staff lived elsewhere, it was to them that the bungalow clearly belonged, on whom its preservation depended, while foreigners came and went.

Yes, Jo had absorbed the change from the false paradise of the field station to the fallen world of a government capital. She waddled around the garden but stayed off the street as Hastings Banda objected to women in drawstring pants, or any pants. At night, the staff gone, her hosts moved to the lounge (more of Her Majesty's cane furniture) where Ian smoked and exchanged telling looks with his wife between lines of conversation. For relaxation, they sampled the radio or played backgammon; Jo might be asked to explain Ronald Reagan, as straight man to the couple's riffing, or she might yawn and go to bed. She was never lonely, yet felt marooned. Her stare, fixed on the garden, or on the pages of journals, might have been the proverbial desert island dweller's waiting for a sail.

The formidable Dr. Emma Baeder, checking Jo over with gloved claws and chill speculum, pronounced her healthy but in need of breath training that must begin immediately at home. Together with Molly (who thought it practical) Jo learned patterned breathing. They practiced the sustained breath, which reminded them of scuba training; the accelerated breath, which got them high; and the variable breath, also called *hee-hee-who*, which Baeder dauntingly called "your breath for severe pain." When Jo had Braxton-Hicks contractions, she would lie in her bedroom and practice. The fetus kicked in its airless sleep, and she wondered what it knew. Her effort not to stroke her belly and talk to it, reassure it of its future, strained her sluggish nerves unbearably.

An American family had been found who were ready to adopt a white baby Malawian. At the clinic, Jo had signed the adoption papers, first asking if she could remain unknown to the family, and they to her. She felt shamed before old Baeder, whose caved cheeks, braided rust-and-steel coiffure, medical whites, and the tiny concession of a fine ladies' wristwatch, put her beyond all moral taint.

"Sure!" Dr. Baeder gave the American word a scrubbing sound. "This is permitted. Also if you would change your mind when the child is born, it is your legal right." The agency records gave Jo an alias, a protocol used to protect women from the stigma of premarital pregnancy. So far, so good, but the revelation that she could still change her mind about adoption, despite the signed papers, gave Jo a splitting headache. She remembered it. Yes, that part of her life was all about the problem of what she might become. Picturing herself with a fat, smiling babe in arms—a single working mother, doughty, devoted—she'd felt a squeezing in her brains. She would be bound to her enemy, and his actions, and the mediocrity he wished on her, for life. But imagining herself slipping into jeans and going to observe her *mwamunas* had brought her the guiltiest of comforts, the breath of freedom.

Out of oblivion flared a conversation—how could she have forgotten! Of course, they had discussed it on the verandah, Molly full of her Chewa proverbs. *Two shelters make you get wet. The monkey fell and died while grabbing for two fruits. Don't stick two fingers in one nostril.* Which choice Molly favored, she was adamant in not telling; she could not live with having swayed her friend one way or another. Jo was left to her own devices, and yearned hopelessly for guidance. Her heart—the vacant heart of the desert island dweller—ached for her mother, dead of unnamed complications.

From childbirth itself, Jo retained some clear memories, and some fragmentary glimpses—like the iron bar, at the foot of her flat, soaked bed, that came to mean the unbending cruelty of the unendurable. The important memory that she'd kept to herself, for thirty-two years, was of seeing her child before she gave it away. When she'd signed the adoption papers, she'd made clear her wish not to see the newborn; she only wanted her body back, and felt, guiltily, that in the circumstances she had no right to see the baby. Labor changed her idea of her rights. To Molly, after it was over, she said just this:

"Guess what? I owe you for saving my life." Molly demurred, of course, as to Jo's debt; but later they set up a fund for the village school attended by Chisomo's niece. This sealed their life-long friendship.

Jo's labor lasted nine hours. She was attended by Dr. Baeder and Grace, a nurse with mighty upper arms and a voice of such melting warmth that at the sound of her saying, "five centi-meet-ahs dila*tion*," the base of Jo's brain felt safe. During the worst, when Grace's voice penetrated Jo's pain saying to push or change position, Jo obeyed her, and when Grace said, "God is helping you," Jo believed her. That was the best of giving birth in Malawi, in an expensive private facility that lacked adjustable beds, wasn't set up for epidurals, reeked of carbolic acid wafted by stuttering fans, and entertained some hens by the entrance as if to remind her how much safer reproduction was for birds.

She spent the first stage in a ward with three other patients, whom she knew only as a pair of silences and a chatter irrelevant as a parrot's, outside her blue mosquito netting. Carbolic acid's timewarpy odor pressed into her pores. As lengthier contractions wrung her spine, she walked, leaning on Grace's bosom, into a room by herself—a luxury of rich world proportions; at the district hospital they gave birth in rows. Here the heavy work began. Dr. Baeder, injecting her with novocaine, performed a deft epi-siotomy that left Jo hopeful about her pain. In advance, she had declined chloroform and skirmished with Molly, who accused her of craving self-imposed Catholic penances. Jo insisted: she'd gone through hell and wanted the reward of knowing what the big deal was. Now the revelation began.

With each contraction, a serrated blade sawed through gut to spine. With each sustained breath, she seized the end of this deadly thing and pushed it down toward the birth canal, pushed, as it ripped and flashed in her entrails, countless times. Each time was a separate life. Each lifetime of pain stretched longer, while Emma Baeder's face, in a spotless cap, popped up past the curve of Jo's belly and glared like a research satellite.

"Push push push push push, " ordered Baeder with scrubbing sounds. "Stop! You must stop! Rest!" Each order was echoed in the nurse's warm voice. But there was no rest.

"Faster breathe! Push push push push! Do not stop breathing!" Sweating buckets from her face, Jo felt a cold sponge at her temples. "Knees up!" barked Baeder. Enormous pressure was building in her spine, as if it were being rolled aside by a slow explosion. Knees to chest she pushed against the crawling sawblade, countless times. Each time was a separate life. Each lifetime of explosive pain lasted on and on, and in one of them the lovely voice praised her and she gasped,

"Give me gin!"

The tired nurse laughed; the hand on Jo's belly, light as a giant moth, gave her a pat. The other hand tipped a paper cup of water between her lips. Contractions stabbed through the coccyx; water spilled from her mouth. Jo went back on the job. The job suddenly got much harder; within the cavity of her being everything was eyes being dragged from their sockets. Black mist filled her sight. Baeder made a sound and plastic was slapped on her face. She fell out of her mind. The lights were back on, she was in the room, Grace was with her, the pain was too—but the pain was now a big gray fist making vague motions; she saw it trying to impress her, a big dustball shooed out from under a bed, stinky too. Jo, who thought it had been about to kill her, gasped and heard her own laughter pealing from above. Grace patted her again. Gradually, the job changed. She entered the ring of fire; she stopped laughing; her birth canal stretched around a white-hot branding iron the diameter of an infant and her breathing rhythm collapsed.

"Crowning," the doctor reported sharply. "Do not push! Breathe! The baby comes!"

"Head is out, breathe now," said Grace. But the ring of fire, the final pain lasting only a few seconds, stretched. Jo huffed the variable breath of last resort. *Hee-hee-who!* The doctor's head popped up and stared with eyes reflective as copper, in deep white sockets. "The right shoulder is stuck," Baeder announced, "on the pelvic bone. Pressure," she ordered. Grace immediately leaned over and dug her fist, wrapped in her other hand, into Jo's pubic skin; while the ultimate pain, the almost end, usurped the next few seconds, and the next few, setting fire to time. Instead of the baby coming out, Baeder's claw went in. Jo howled in anguish. She was told to push.

"God is helping you," called the beautiful voice. *Hee-hee-who!*

"*So*," grunted Baeder, and stood up, a newborn arm in her right hand and the attached baby in her left, as if the dripping baby had flung out an arm to drag itself from the deep.

Afterwards, Jo awoke in a fog of mosquito netting, unsure of time and place, with a pair of conversations carried on around her. Just out of earshot, two women were murmuring; one a visitor, and the other, in a playful whine, complaining. English syllables dangled at random from the murmur like dewdrops. In the direction of Jo's feet, another pair of women traded remarks in Chewa.

"Hey," Jo called, in a voice whose weakness scared her, but the murmurers heard.

"Nurse! Nurse!" they cried, indignant. "Don't you hear? You're wanted!"

Grace thrust her head between the folds of the mosquito netting. Her white cap, and the light behind her, made Jo's eyes creak.

"Where's my baby? I want to see the baby." Speech was an athletic feat. Grace hurriedly took pulse and temperature, explaining as the glass thermometer jarred Jo's teeth that she would ask the doctor. She turned, raising the thermometer to the light outside, and closed the netting. The other conversation had fallen into bossy silence.

"*Zimachitika* . . ." sighed Grace, as her footsteps scuffed away. It was what Winton said when equipment broke, or Chisomo,

when monkeys raided the fruit. It was the expression on everyone's lips after a death in the village. Molly called it the essence
of Malawian fatalism, because it meant, *this happens*. The visitor
made sounds of preparing to leave; there were whispers, then
the complainer's bedclothes rustled briefly. The mosquito netting
around Jo's bed swelled like the lining of a dark cloud. An epoch
stretched. The cloud parted and was swept aside; the swaddled
infant, whose head filled Grace's palm, was laid in Jo's reaching
arms. Its fists were pink snails, its mouth a tidepool flower. Jo held
it to her face, sniffed its crown, and the front of her coarse gown
spotted wet. Her nipples were crying or laughing. She thought, I
have put my mother back in the world.

"He is healthy," said the lovely voice. Jo looked up at Grace.
The nurse's eyes, in her full-chinned face, were simple and alert.
They did not mirror Jo's astonishment that she had produced a
male. The spirit figure of a little girl in starched skirts had given
way to this, a reality Jo had never bargained for; outsize head,
wrapped boy-baby, warmth to die for. She hesitated to speak,
but Grace, needing no prompt, said she might wait a few days
before the final step; mothers of newborns sometimes changed
their minds. Breast-feeding would help the baby's immunities,
the nurse suggested.

Jo bared her breast, and with some assistance the baby latched
onto her and suckled. She was as amazed as if a conjuror, whisk-
ing away a satin cloak, had changed her into the Madonna. This
was what the big deal was. This core of love. Tiered candles el-
evated her; prayers reached her from the pit of night. Then, as
the baby whimpered and squawked, handing him back to Grace
to be burped—woozy with love, and appalled with questions—Jo
made up her mind.

As it happened, Dr. Baeder had come in to check her stitches, and learning that the baby had sucked a dose of colostrum,
was not displeased. Unlike her staff, old Baeder showed no more
signs of tiring than the elements. She reported that the stitches
looked good, but since Jo's torn vagina had needed forty-three of
them, she would have to rest and postpone travel. Both doctor

and nurse watched Jo with careful neutrality; not for the world would they lay a feather's weight on the scale of her decision. Yet she knew that the instant she said aloud "my son," making him hers, both of these impeccable professionals would break into smiles of a very special regard. Then she would forever have another life.

She spoke up in her weak voice. Baeder nodded, took the slightly hiccupping infant from Grace, lifted it onto a bony shoulder and said to it, "Hopla!" She promised to discharge Jo within the next twenty-four hours if all went well. Jo scarcely heard her. As the doctor took her baby, he'd pulled with him the breast he'd sucked, detaching it with ropy, fat-flocked vessels and lump of heart, now dangling like afterbirth between Jo's open chest and Baeder's shoulder—a crisis, a medical emergency. But Baeder left, the baby with her.

Jo cried out to Grace, who was rearranging her bedclothes, begging the nurse to unhook the gold cross from around her neck and put it on the baby. Grace tucked her patient in and stood facing her, arms folded, half compassion, half cool reason. To put gold on a baby would invite thieves. But Jo was desperate to send some talisman of love with her son, some part of her he would keep. At last, Grace fetched a comb and scissors. She combed out Jo's tangled hair, her fingers weaving in it. There were two tugs, and a snip. Before Jo's eyes, with amused satisfaction, Grace held up the plaited lock knotted midway and at both ends. Jo calmed down as if by magic. Grace hunted up a coin envelope that the clinic could spare, and the plait, snugly fitting it, was sealed in for its journey. Jo sighed.

"*Zikomo kwambiri,*" she said, the finest thanks she could almost pronounce. "I will remember."

"*Zikomo,*" Grace replied—since it also meant "you're welcome"—and wished Jo luck. Her shift was over, and they would not see each other again.

"Am I a monster?" Jo impulsively asked Dr. Baeder the next day, during her discharge interview, as she drew on her pants and the now oversize man's shirt she'd bought in San Diego. It was

uneasy moment to remember. Baeder had said no—just "No"—
as if responding to a literal question about the number of Jo's
heads, while slipping a phial of tablets into a take-away bag of
sanitary supplies. From the same hand that had reached into Jo's
bleeding birth canal, delivered her baby, then carried her baby
away, Jo accepted the paper bag. Her stitches looked good, but
her brief exposure to nitrous oxide (which Baeder did not deign
to call laughing gas) meant she would need a follow-up. Jo shook
the veinous hand whose grip was stone.

Baeder then gave her a look it had taken decades to decipher.
The doctor's deep, grizzled sockets held a gaze of copper that
seemed to tilt, like fish eyes, as they registered her. In retrospect,
it was the assessing look of large experience. Then, having said
all she expected Jo to comprehend, Dr. Baeder wished her best
of luck.

*   *   *

If she'd learned one thing from childbirth, it was that the key
to surviving pain was focus. This lesson suited Jo's love of prob-
lem-solving; eventually, the episode of her pregnancy had boiled
down (as she would say) to being distracted, in the sense of driven
to distraction. Never again would her mind be so strange as in
that time of madness and sorrow.

Over the years, she'd also suspected that if she cared to examine the past, a twinge of unfinished business lurked in it. Truth
to tell, though, Jo was much more interested in other animals
than in herself. If she'd had more sense of irony, she might have
exercised it on the fact that *M. mowae*, the subject of her early discovery, was now the *sine qua non* behind her painful self-discovery
during the night hours in her office. She had no taste, though, for
paradoxes. Having come so far, remembering all that could be
remembered, she felt she gripped the unfinished business by its
root. She plucked it up. She had started by asking how she could
have *a lot in common* with a monster like Lewis Everett. Face it, she
told herself now: in her own mind, rightly or wrongly, their com-

mon ground was the rejection of a son. Leo, in all ignorance, had
pierced thirty years of defenses against the rage she'd suppressed;
it had gushed forth at the prick to her ancient guilt. That was
the root she'd plucked up—the problem of being a monster. She
had never believed Emma Baeder's *no*, which was why the doctor,
knowingly, hadn't seen fit to elaborate.

Baeder, surely dead, had foreseen the tears Jo shed tonight.
Was she done? Could she go home now?

Something still lurked. Near midnight (how near she didn't
care) her powers of intuition woke. When she worked hard at
a certain level of a problem, only to have her conclusions strike
her as preliminary, it was a dead giveaway that they were preliminary. Her mind moved now without help of words or images, in a
sphere of logic all its own, dark and clear, like the universe before
stars. She was at home here: this was her true home.

She seemed asleep in her chair: slight, ashen, still. Then, as if
a statue jumped into a getaway car, Jo whirled toward her computer monitor, brilliant with wet greens and browns. It was morning at the water hole, and juvenile elephants stroked each other's
heads with their trunks. Ordinarily this scene would have delight-
ed her. Jo banished it and looked up Leo Jaeger's birth date.

"Hunh," she exhaled. "Thank God. Thank God." Her voice
fell strangely on the air that expected to convey only the night
sounds of machines. She checked her Apple watch automatically.
It was time to go.

She rose, stretched disgruntled muscles, discarded the napkins,
and without switching on the lights (not to disturb the fish) found
her shoes. The chair Leo had occupied, face in his hands, was at a
restless angle to her desk. She rolled it straight and held onto the
vinyl back, while the bolt of fear she'd just experienced reverber-
ated in simultaneous visions of Leo's grand blond body weighing
on her own, sheathed inside her, and the convulsive anguish as
her baby was tugged out of her. Thank God not. Thank God not
true. Her heart jogged and thumped offbeat. Without a thought,
she breathed in the way she'd learned years ago; deep, sustained
breaths. On the other end of her breath was the force that had

sawed with its serrated sword in her gut, that time—then it had been pain, now it was memory, and now she understood there were no monsters in her life. There was only survival. This was not a heart attack, she was doing fine.

"Okay," Jo whispered, passing a hand over her chest. Luxuriously, she breathed in without the answering pressure. She'd been stressed, that was all. But now she felt free.

Closing her office door behind her, she had an impulse to visit the mowae. She needed a walk, and the fish rooms were in a building not far from the lab. Outside, the campus walkways were adequately lit though the sky was dark and crickets pulsed. Pedestrians were about, some in lab coats, some walking their bicycles toward the avenue. The cool air smelled as if the past day had been wrapped in layers of eucalyptus-scented tissue. Jo felt refreshed, and during the long, steep escalator ride down to the fish rooms, enjoyed her body's balance. On the lowest floor, she shoved open a heavy door and was enveloped in the moist whale's-breath of the fish rooms, much warmer than the lab. Jo made her way through rooms of metal stacks filled with, not books, but plastic containers in which dark specks swam. A few techs, working late, waved as she passed through. Shrimp churned like meal in the tall incubation tanks, and the air shook with the pumps' rhythm; a hand laid on the fish room walls would feel the vibration of channeled waters. At the threshold of the mowae's room, Jo paused, about to enter and be immersed in acoustic bubbles issuing from the tanks, mounted four rows deep around the walls. The cement floor shone in streaks where excess water had been mopped. Jo's full lips parted in something like mute prayer. Index cards were clipped to the tanks, along with maintenance checklists, and Leo was reading them, his pale hair astir like anemone in the grayish light. He wore his lab coat and his big brown Crocs.

She was tempted to leave, to change nothing in the scene that fulfilled her wish. But she walked in, and at the sound of her heels, Leo turned, an index card in his blue-gloved hand.

"See," he said when she joined him. "Animal Care's furious because this card wasn't updated. I'm having to double-check all the cards, because the techs don't do their job. Plus, there was water all over the floor. No shit," he stressed mildly. On his nape, a few stars of sweat crawled as he displayed the card for Jo. After a moment's thought, she promised to look into it, and suggested that they check the tanks' acidity.

It was almost midnight. They worked side by side, Jo taking the lower tanks and Leo the upper. His broad wrist, and her thin one, executed the selfsame gesture of dipping a paper slip and holding it level as it changed color. Meanwhile, they talked in a desultory way about Leo's idea of putting a ten-foot tank in the middle of the room. The giant tank would be "visually impactful," he said, and in the presence of rivals, the male mowae would display their health with vivid colors and drama. Jo called it a good idea, but, she warned, they'd have to prevent the males from massacring each other while the conference people were viewing them. Territories would have to be accounted for, when the tank was hardscaped.

"See that?" she pointed. Holding a Quick-Dip level in midair, Leo torqued his body to view the tank beneath, where a small male cowered inside a bit of PVC pipe while a big male flashed between its exits, scowling like a dragon.

"They're mean fish," he agreed. "They love to hate."

The scientists stepped back and surveyed the animals whose genetic doom they had lifted. Each tank held two males swishing darkly around, as if fleeing their trailing fins, and a group of orange-ish females. They weren't at their colorful best in this light, yet the sight of them all at once, ceaselessly circulating, gave Jo a slow thrill of revelation. These were the males doomed to die young, the females doomed to search endlessly for scarce mates—and they could not have looked more energetic. It came to her that their fate, a species' immemorial fate, had been removed from their wonderful bodies. But that's it, she thought, that's the meaning. Nothing is like this. Nothing that is, or has gone before, is like what I see in this room. Her collaborator changed his nitrile gloves, wincing when they pulled hairs.

"Can I assume," she asked, "you're back?"

Fluorescent light turned Leo's narrow eyes brown as he caught hers and returned to the tanks, Jo following.

"Yeah, I went home and saw my folks," he said. "They keep bees. Eight hives this year. Dad needed to find one of his queens, and since I'm the biologist—but as you know, Jo, I have trouble telling my own fish apart. Mol bio is not fieldwork."

"You do okay." On the tank's glass wall, their reflections blended.

"There was this cloud of smoke and bees," Leo gesticulated. "I got stung twice by the same bee, which doesn't happen?"

"Very rarely if they're stinging a mammal," Jo qualified. "Our skin is too thick."

"Right. We couldn't find the queen," Leo resumed, "because she wasn't marked, and an unmarked queen's hard to spot. But Dad said she was in there, so I kept trying to look with smoke blowing in my face. There were these masses of confused, angry bees crawling around, and one got inside my sleeve and I tried to shake it loose, and it stung me. Twice. Man! All I could think of was how much I wanted—my father not to go home disappointed." On the tank, through their reflections' shadow, swam and wove the mowae, rust-red, bruise-blue.

"You're a good son," Jo said. "Did you find the queen?"

Leo gave his playful bark of a laugh, which she hadn't heard for centuries. "We did! Let me show you something." From his coat pocket, Leo brought out his iPhone and fiddled with its settings, his vitreous eyebrows working. "It's at home. My folks sent a photo." He offered up the phone, and Jo took it, cocking her head.

"Anything but a sick fish," joked the PI, expecting a long-bellied queen bee. She held the device closer, then farther, squinting. Then she spread the tips of thumb and forefinger on the screen, as if parting closed eyelids, and studied the enlarged image.

"This was sent with my adoption paperwork," Leo explained. "It's from the birth mother. Jo, the whole time I was trying to drag some kind of concession out of Everett, I had this from whomever who gave me my life." Nested in tissue, a knotted silk cord; no, a hair extension in unreal platinum blond. "I think it means, she gave me what she could. And you were right. I need to give what I can."

The fall of Jo's ashen hair hid her expression. Then she coughed, and one hand rose to her throat. The full lips were drawn, the pallor abrupt. The room's bubbling grew louder and louder until she produced, in her throat, a click, and seemed shocked at her voicelessness.

She hissed, "Sorry—" and threw Leo a look like a deep sea anchor, a look no power could dislodge, before heading out of the room at a taut clip.

"Are you okay?" Leo called after her. He sent a text. Then he returned to catching up with routine maintenance, trusting that the PI would check back later.

In one of the tanks, he was pleased to see the most telling sign of the mowae's vigor: a mating dance. An orange female circled in iridescent indecision. Below her, a male shivered against the current, face set in a paranoid pout, exhibiting his sunny dorsal fin, his midnight body, his fascinating egg-spots. Leo grinned. Who could ask for more?

* * *

There came a moment when her will surrendered, her body doubled over the restroom toilet, just after a keen terror that organ tissues were leaving her mouth. In blackness marbled with green stars, palms against a wall she no longer saw, an image rose. A round metal lid embossed with a dolphin. Her mind rested, recognizing the drain cover of an outlet to the Bay. In that moment, she accepted her body's authority to live or die, continue or dissolve. The eye of time's storm turned around her.

In the first hour of the morning, her body recomposed, and her mind witnessed trembling, soreness, stink, bile, tears. The future's weight settled on her, weak though she was. At length, she found water, soap, paper towels, mints, and cleansed herself with wonderment at her skill, as if she were speaking forgotten high school French. In the mirror, finally, she looked kempt and old.

Leaving the women's restroom, she entered the L-shaped hallway. Her office was around the corner. She stood in the long hall,
facing the shut laboratory door. Someone was in there. She knew
by instinct, and what was more, she smelled fresh coffee from
the urn outside her office, a few steps away; sure enough, it was
warm. In the pale fluorescence, she filled a paper cup. When she
drank, a chemical chord sounded from sole to crown: here I *am*.

"Ah," Jo said, restored to herself. Her baby was safe. Her duty
was to keep the secret of his birth. She must let Leo become, as
before, her collaborator and ex-lover: the rest was silence. Was
she strong enough? She must be. Sure, or she would have passed
out in the fucking women's restroom. She drank a second cup
of coffee, stirring into it all the available sugar packets. Having
slaked thirst and hunger, the PI went to see which night owl was
puttering around in Mayhew Lab.

The lab was divided into five bays, like fingers on a hand,
each defined by the parallel benches at which a pair of scientists
worked back to back. Connecting all the bay's entrances was a
lane where Jo walked, looking into each bay as she passed by the
freezers, centrifuges, incubators, and other equipment in common use. The first bay, Ilya's, was empty, as expected. Faint human sounds led her into the third bay, where Pradeep, propped
swaybacked between his arms, his fingers splayed, neck lolling,
black hair falling forward as if desperate for a pillow, peered into
a benchtop transilluminator.

Poor Pradeep. He was devoted to the spores of an ancient
bacterium discovered inside salt crystals, in a core sample from
the bed of the Southern Ocean. The spores had inspired him
because they were alive. But they were also almost half a billion
years old, surrounded by their fossilized relatives. Pradeep had
spent over a year vainly trying to grow these beings of time's
abyss, while his grant money dwindled and the lab joked about
Sleeping Beauty bugs.

"What's up?" Jo asked. "Anything?"

Her heels' tapping made her entrance noticeable, but he was
oblivious. Then he welcomed her with shimmering anxiety, want-

ing to show her his latest gel. He poured forth an explanation about a sample from an anaerobic jar—he used several culture methods but only the jars seemed to be taking right now, in low concentrations, that is, fairly low concentrations, but the point is they were *there*, and this time, contamination was out of the question, absolutely. He had to stop talking when a yawn broke in.

"Where?" Jo asked, bent over the transilluminator, a shallow lightbox. Against the background's blue glow appeared the DNA markers, in scuffed lines of neon green. Pradeep's fingertip hovered.

"There, if you look very closely."

"The most overused words in mol bio are 'if you look very closely.'" Beside her, Pradeep emitted prayerful energies. She blinked hard and looked again at the DNA markers of microscopic life from under the bed of an ocean, from inside salt crystals, from an age when oxygen was unimportant. "Well . . . yes, I think I see what you're seeing." If it's replicable, she added privately, and not contamination again.

But it was obvious that she'd made his (extremely long) day, and they discussed the gel. Pradeep noticed that Jo seemed different: more relaxed, somehow, but under the weather, as if she'd come in with a cold. Her nose and eyes were red. He hoped it wasn't a cold, as the very idea of getting sick at this crucial time exasperated him; strategically, he inquired after her health, and pronounced himself glad to know she was well. She gleamed at him like a terrier that has guessed where the rat is.

Embarrassed, he suddenly recalled that he'd wanted to ask her about the FOIA request. He didn't want to get bad news right now, but having thought of it, he couldn't bear the suspense. "About this FOIA situation . . ."

"No worries!" She could be as graceful as a girl, with a slender-wristed gesture. "It's going right back up the pipeline. Stanford is good at that."

"I wish I understood why our government is not good at it, I mean at protecting scientists from these weird sorts of attacks. One would like to think that America is America," Pradeep said.

Jo concurred, and they entertained each other with outrageous tales of public and official ignorance. Pradeep had heard a talk show host who had said that since scientists changed their minds, but the Bible didn't, the Bible was more reliable. They bemoaned talk shows, creationist museums, and Congress. With the happy animation of a man whose fears are flown, Pradeep asked Jo about her gold cross. He was merely curious, with respect, of course, to know, was it hard reconciling her faith and her work?

She was leaning against his bench, her navy pencil skirt creased between her hip bones, careful not to brush against the anaerobic jars. As she touched her cross, she looked down, chin nestling in tough folds that told her age. She was a mixture, Pradeep thought, of preserved youthfulness and polished climacteric. Ageless for a moment.

"I'm a pretty bad Catholic, I guess. This belonged to my mother. I always forget I'm wearing it. I suppose by now it's more of a symbol of my mother than God."

"Mothers and gods, who can tell the difference," Pradeep quavered. They laughed, but Jo shook her sleek gray head.

"Mothers are animals like everyone else. I think," she went on, seeing his slight shock, "maybe one reason we're up against this FOIA craziness, and the climate change deniers, and everything you and I have just been complaining about, is that people lose track of that very simple fact."

"I'm not sure what you mean?"

Jo felt tempted to ask this researcher into life's ancestry if he'd ever learned the details of his own birth. But her sense of propriety held, and she returned their conversation to the DNA markers in the bluely lit transilluminator.

Meanwhile, sadness sighed louder than usual in the eaves of her mind; it whispered of how she had learned to imagine her mother as a saint in heaven, and had never guessed what *complications* meant until she'd been torn and stitched back together, complicating (yes truly) her life with internal scars and a secret son. She would always remember yearning for her mother, before the birth. How had her mother encountered the sword in her gut, the force carving out of you the strength you would pass on? That force was natural selection—not an idea, she knew: an experience. Evolution took its course through the experience of billions of mothers.

Here was memory's core: the sunlit workroom, smelling of mist, formaldehyde and moist brick. The burbling tanks. And herself, decentered by the heavy unwanted baby, observing the wild females spit out their eggs, curvetting in piscine fury. The fish refused their offspring out of stress; Jo had traded hers for freedom, and both these choices were animal, made by females seeking a way to survive. She'd believed she was a monster when she'd been ridden by shame, guilt, and isolation; she had believed it forever, though less so tonight. Would that her mother had been remembered as a woman struggling for life, not as a skiing angel. But in her childhood, she knew—for her own intended good—the glory of eternal souls had been held up to dazzle and distract from the truth of her animal being. She forgave the church only to spare herself more loss. And she recalled Everett, the collector of scientific antiquities, reviling her *sainted little girl parts*. Well, she'd taken his job. A few hundred little boys were at risk for CMTX6, in California; they might not be her sons, but they and Leo were the heirs of her discovery.

Jo advised Pradeep to recalibrate the spectrophotometer regularly, and said good night. As she left, he thought he heard her odd chuckle. Jo was saying to herself, *zimachitika.*

PART 2

On a hilltop before dawn, in mist and drizzle, a man was due to meet a mountain lion. The lion was slinking around the border of its range. The dirt smelled of cow dung, but the lion had little hope on that score, because it stank of people, too.

From the sky, veils of cloud slanted like leaves in a book. When the last leaf turned, sunlight would show the hills in green winter, the red-tiled roofs of campus, and the flat sheen of the bay.

Meanwhile, Hoover Tower shed a fogged orange glow, and in rifts of mist, a submerged twinkling went on where researchers were still on the cusp of something. The man had been one of them. He'd been accused of working ridiculous hours, breaking with the rich casualness of the valley. But to a stranger's eye, the book of mists would seem to be in its first chapter, without division between world and beast, or beast and human.

The man wore a soggy hoodie and jeans, and moccasins in which his flattish feet had pounded the three miles from the Dish Loop security gate. No one was up here—he'd counted on it, as far as he'd been able to count, untrained in desperation as he was in running. Hair dangled in his eyes. He was running from the laboratory he loved, running from his life as if he were running for it. He was in a state that makes thoughts of suicide irrelevant.

The lion spotted him from the hilltop, which was fenced. It was the lion's habit to circle the fence, smear its cheek along the posts, and hunt for rabbits and squirrels that popped out, or tried to jump inside. Inside the fence stood a gigantic object stranger than anything else in the lion's world. Though the big cat could easily have leapt the fence, it avoided the hilltop because of the object, as well as a building that smelled of humans and attracted them.

Now the lion froze, looking down at a tree under which the man stood, puffing.

The man had run the hard trail to control the arrhythmia of his mind. In extremity, he sought measure. From under a small oak, without hope, he looked up at the gigantic Dish. As he ceased panting, he heard birds. Like steam from wet wood on a fire, a few whistles rose from gauzed-over vales and erased hillsides. The sun was expected to rise soon.

The lion felt curious about the tall man under the tree; it also felt tense and playful, in the manner of cats. Its ears flattened and flicked up. It whistled: a clear, loud chirrup.

The whistle startled the man's imagination, which produced, on the spot, without his awareness, the silver, golden, fiery bird whose myth inhabits our bones, and he was seized with desire to see the calling bird. He'd rarely dealt with whole animals; when he needed mice, he sent an order to the lab manager for mouse tissue that came in a box. The only animals he'd needed to know were those whose genes he repaired. Yet that loud, flashing call, so near, raised in him the winged and brilliant specter of redemption. He began walking toward the lion.

At the pace of his squelching footsteps, the wires between fence posts made deeper scratches in the mist. The man looked up to the dimension of winged creatures. Gradually he made out the Dish's openwork, and the twin ramps, like a sphinx's forelegs, laid on the rails of its circular track. His head fell back, the hood's knot tightening, as he took in the massive radiotelescope, one hundred and fifty feet across, symmetrically constructed as a snowflake, tipped toward the rest of the universe. It was etched in cloud and scarcely visible; most of it was in his mind. He scanned for a bird, but there was none.

Lowering his gaze, he saw, instead, something like a white butterfly, hovering not thirty feet away near a fence post. On either side of the butterfly appeared two black spots. Then the weaving saunter of the white face, with its dark eyes—the sole gleaming things in the vaporous scene—and the separation of a creature, a large creature, from the mists . . . all these cues whirled into the knowledge that he faced a mountain lion, and the normally shy beast was not afraid of him.

Alone and weaponless, he saw the lion's paws, broader than its legs, lifting and falling, but crushed his impulse to flee: two leaps would put it on his back. He raised both arms over his head and tried to shout, but fear wrung his throat.

The young man facing the lion, hands in the air, had run this far because his mind was split: one part clung to his past, the other writhed in a raw present. Now a third mind bloomed. It encompassed the undulating lion, the birds shaking off sleep, the short grim oak at his back. Then the third mind telescoped into action.

He reached into his front pocket, unclipped the phone inside, and let it fly with a shocking yell. The missile crunched somewhere near the beast. The face winked out, and the creature's tail-tip flared darkly, as the half-seen, half-suspected bulk of its body glided back along the fence and dissolved. It was no more to be seen.

He stared till his eyes fairly cracked, scared to leave, scared to move. Time passed; the young man in the desperate situation was not counting. Nothing counted. The hilltop seemed to pale. The Dish, steel lace in the clouds, turned less tricky to see. A long halloo rose from down below, Caltrain on its way to San Francisco. The man felt cold.

At last, he sidled back to the oak tree and went around it, where he couldn't see the Dish. It felt good to piss there, by his tree, on whose bark he laid a hand as his trickle went down and joined the roots. Nothing he felt was in words yet. He walked to the dirt path beside the fence, where he'd seen the lion crouching. Squatting there, he moved crabwise on his haunches a few feet in either direction. Once he looked up and saw the world pearled to the most beautiful blankness he'd ever seen. While he'd been looking in the dirt, dawn had come. The mist was milk. He could see the path bent around the hill; and at his feet, now, he found the lion's print. It seemed filled with transparency.

Inside the paw print, his floating fingers measured the slope dug by the heel pad. Deep in his mind the pleasant thrill awoke that he'd had as a boy, in the fossil quarry where he'd first searched like this, tallying centimeters with his fingertips. Lovingly (for a true sign evoked his love, regardless) he traced the pad's outline, three lobes like linked u's. That was a mountain lion. And the toes: no claw-dots, only four shapely tears. Estimating weight and size, he surveyed the path again, the chain of scuffs, and noted the distance between them. A male, formidable. He sighed.

Then in the grass (at this hour, not blades of green but hemlock-colored fur) he caught the sheen of his iPhone. He cleaned it on his sweatshirt, but couldn't read it; in the luminous softness, the screen didn't meet its right refractive index.

Shading the phone with a hand, he knelt on one knee, and photographed the paw print. He checked the image: perfect, proof of a mountain lion for all to see. But to whom should he send it?

At this thought, the man's new, third mind—which had strengthened his throwing arm, fueled his furious yell, and filled him afterwards with calm—abandoned him. He was seized in the torture-cleft of his split mind again.

Anyone on the hilltop might have seen the tall figure's fists bundle into the hoodie's pocket. Blindly, he cast back for that third mind—painless, even blissful—that he'd had a moment ago. Oak, path, paw print. The anguish stood off slightly. He did it again: tree, path, print. But the third mind lasted only as long as its memories; afterward, pain loomed. Sanity had no staying power. He went rigid, fists in his belly, agonizing over the path that had led from past to present, from that reality to this. It wasn't as if he had purposely committed a crime for which he could atone. He could have lived with that. But it was dumb luck that had steered him wrong. Luck was the path between realities. As he knew, he knew—he'd always said evolution was about luck, which was fine until this hilltop encased in mist, where absolute loneliness was breathing on him. He belonged to nothing he recognized anymore. He had left the human circle, and his pain, moment by moment, felt inhuman.

In his lab was a refrigerator that he would now be opening if his real life were restored. Inside its glass door, slightly misted, on crowded shelves stood his racked test tubes, color-coded with stripes and dots of tape. In each cloudy tube grew a strain of bacteria whose genes he had synthesized. Creatures without parents, their roots in his nitrile-gloved hands. He'd always felt a calm, generous sense of power, opening the door. Every day, he set about repairing a point mutation in the human genome, using synthetic DNA. Ultraviolet light had smashed up some wildly distant human ancestor's gene. Wham out of the void of space had come a lineage of human suffering. He had discovered the damaged gene, and a way to heal the effects of that smash-up for future generations. He had replaced dumb luck with skill, cosmic randomness with reason. He belonged in the lab. He did not deserve to be cold through and through because of what, like thunder vibrating in the ground, made his thoughts stumble.

He crouched by the path and gazed at the paw-print, in which thin shadows were swimming, and ached to send his picture. On a sunny day, he could see the lab building from here. If his life were restored, right now, he could touch Send, and he'd be hearing back from Ilya, Pradeep, Eero at the med school, all those guys. Into his daydream rose a white-coated woman at a coffee urn.

He'd never been a careless person, but the hand of luck had spilled him in her path like a mutagen. Sins could be forgiven, crimes could be punished, but what was the cure for monstrosity? Never had he imagined. He'd grown up knowing that the story of his birth was sealed in darkness. As a boy, he'd suffered the strange loneliness of it; he'd imagined finding and rescuing a lost woman from whatever had kept them apart. By now, the rift between his adult self and his animal beginnings in some unknown, long-ago belly was no more to him, and no less, than the Hadean darkness at the root of all life. Never had he imagined and he had to stop there, stop the memory of, the thought of, touching a woman. He stopped. But the moment did not stop. The moment when he'd done it to—her, himself—and when he'd guessed what he'd, they'd done—were the same moment, and the same as now. His heart kept beating into the same moment. Any action he took, even his sleep, was locked in the same moment. The moment when his beginning snaked around and latched its jaws onto his end. The wrong he'd done rolled on and on. He had no way forward that was not back. And he had no way back. He was forever in the moment when he'd accidentally committed the wrong that only a human could commit, because only a human could find himself changed into a beast.

He dug for his car keys; the damp pocket was disgraceful, as were the moccasins in which his feet coldly stewed. He imagined jogging downhill, miles in the mist, to the parking lot, to go away forever. Words twitched on his lips, and just then a bird called—a clear, loud chirrup.

This time he knew, as if he'd magically summoned it, the lion snarling on the bend of the path. Gashed throat, blood springing in the dirt, legs and arms higgedly-piggedly dragged off and gnawed: the young man foresaw his future. It unrolled before him as, fallen on his knees, he heard the mountain lion whistle and could not move.

Another whistle replied, less distinctly.

He heard them all around him now. With the wind from below, from the gray valley, blowing on the direction of his thoughts, he followed their calls. Some were closer, some farther—some right beside him. Common yellowthroats were calling their territories. Towhees exchanged metallic chirps between mates. Scrub jays spoiled for a fight. Robins caroled at points near and far among the hills, where in some hidden fold the lion denned down in sleep. Their singing no lion's cruel whistle but the dawn chorus. The danger was past. His limbs trembled, his tears were loosened. *Here, here,* they called, here among them, lucky animal, he belonged to life! And from the root system of his nerves swept an exultation that consumed everything he was and recomposed him, glowing.

He regained his feet, whispering swears. He wiped his streaming eyes, wiped back his hair, and for the last time, looked up at the Dish. Now the mists, drawn toward the sky's shining and somber cloud-wrack, wreathed around and wafted up through the radiotelescope. The sight was as stern and gorgeous as a Bible picture, a ladder for angels. It was also dear and ordinary. As he gazed, his body felt altered. Something missing, a missing pressure, made him feel lighter. . . . The horror of his monstrosity, the torture of his split mind, were not in him now . . . purged in the passage from mortal fear to the wild high of escape. Finding himself safe, he found a different self.

At this moment, he thought, the Dish might be communicating with a space probe on the edge of the solar system. He was a scientist; and an animal, too, among the rest, ruled by luck and oh man lucky. Birds were calling. Something entered him that was not pain or the absence of pain, but a quiet, lasting wonder.

BEDCRUMBS

Where there are sheets there is lint. You may sleep on cotton
with a thread count so high it's practically marble, but you cannot avoid friction (if you're reading this, you don't want to) and
that produces, inevitably, lint. Where there is lint, there are bedcrumbs. Some people don't like the thought of cohabiting wil-
ly-nilly with microlife, but in my opinion such people are delud-
ed in the belief that their bodies are private property. When my
eyelashes brush my lover's cheek, it's the spires on the homes of
follicle mites bringing that sleepy smile to his face. Adorable creatures, the mites in our eyelash follicles! Like St. Thomas Aquinas'
angels, they do not crap, wasting so little that Nature hasn't even
troubled to fit their wee behinds with orifices for that purpose;
and more usefully than angels, they eat our dead skin cells. They
groom us, hurt no one, foul nothing, and live like so many peaceful hobbits in a snug row of holes, their doors repainted whenever
we apply eyeshadow.

Bedcrumbs affect us more than eyelash mites. Your sudden
craving for a particular snack or drink after sex is the work of
bedcrumbs. This is not the same honest appetite gotten from
working off calories. It starts with a vision of, say, a warm slice of
coffee cake, its pebbled top bursting with butter, the pores of its
sides breathing cinnamon, its treasury of brown sugar clumping
in your teeth, then dissolved in coffee. . . . You flip over onto your
bedmate's chest, interrupting his snores; you fold a leg over his
dreaming privates, lace your fingers through his lax hand, and
whisper in his ear, "I could really go for some dessert, huh?" Or
it's he who nuzzles your nape, reminiscently tweaks your nipples,
and slides a palm firm with future plans down your belly, murmuring, "I keep thinking about pizza." Neither of you dreams
that your next step toward your vivid vision is controlled by the

mist of lint particles, about fifty microns in diameter, that was stirred up by your amorous exertions.

Inside each cotton particle lives a colony of invisible bacteria: the bedcrumbs. They're saprophytes: they eat dead plant matter. That's why they like lint. Deep inside the particle—which from their perspective is a grand, gloomy, vaulted catacomb—they huddle in an alchemical cabal to produce a special fluid, a weird, arcane chartreuse of a byproduct. This fluid evaporates and is inhaled by our noses, where it makes contact with our two senses of smell: the usual one, and the "vomeronasal organ," which sounds disgusting, but is responsible for our picking up the interesting scents that govern sex. Through these two routes the scent travels straight to our brains where it locks into olfactory memory and activates it such that food is what you remember, but with all the allure of Eros. A memory rises up from your store of victuals past and hovers before your mind's eye, or nose, radiant with afterlove and fanning its wings. At that point you want the perfect snack.

What do plant-eating bacteria gain from making a chemical of weapon-grade sophistication that's useless to them, but triggers human olfactory memories? Bacteria, remember, are no fools. They invented photosynthesis—and in so doing, created an oxygen-filled atmosphere—so it's fair to say that a chemical that messes with human free will is a piece of cake to them, if there's a good reason. And bacteria always have a reason. They may take a few million generations to work through the evolutionary logic, but they always have a reason. Aristotle was dead wrong to call humankind the "rational animal." While we run around forgetting where we put the car keys, losing our tempers, hitting our kids, fighting wars, getting in debt, and generally acting loco, bacteria do exactly, *but exactly*, what it is in their collective self-interest to do. When we beat them, it is with brute chemical force. When they beat us, it's with the light touch of genetic mastery. So simply ask: what do beings living inside bits of dead plants, and eating their way out, want? More and bigger plants. What do you need to make more and bigger plants? Soil nutrients. Where do you get those? Various places, including the decomposing bodies

of animals. What is the best decomposing animal to produce nutrients for more and bigger plants? A big, fat animal. How do you
fatten up a large animal if you're an invisible bacterium that lives
in a fifty-micron ball of lint? Q.E.D.

Another strategy may have evolved simultaneously with the
former. The vision of the perfect mouthful, which propels us
from bed toward the phone and refrigerator, is a gustatory mi-
rage. This world is no five-star restaurant, and the morsel we finally bring to our lips can never equal our ideal. The pizza will
ooze with voluptuousness only to overwhelm us with banality.
The coffee cake won't taste like it should. It will disappoint like a
melody memorized in a dream when you hum it into the morning toothbrush glass. The bedcrumbs may be counting on us to
pine away, deprived of our ideal food, and die off at a faster rate.
Either way, whether we die content and fat, or disillusioned and
thin, the bedcrumbs win. They are bacteria. We are only human.

In the face of such might, it's good to reflect that orgasms are
naturally more perfect than desserts; so as the poets have often
said, let us love each other and stay in bed.

THE GIFTS OF CHEF WANG

The contemporary physicist Roger Penrose has declared himself unhappy with the whole gamut of interpretations of Heisenberg's principle. . . .
Jim Holt, in *Slate*, March 6, 2002

The weaver-god, he weaves, and by that weaving is he deafened that he hears no mortal voice.
Herman Melville, *Moby-Dick*

We all know how science, these days, is guided by the interests of billionaires, some rather eccentric. Time travel was developed just because and tested just once, on a Canadian who'd sold his business for the price of a trip. The Canadian vanished; his family brought a killer lawsuit, and Chef Wang, scenting opportunity, bought the patent right—risky tech, legal tangles and all—for a song. The Penrose time travel system (named for the trailblazing Roger Penrose) was installed in a walk-in cooler, and top-flight scientists were hired by the Great Leap Restaurant Company.

You may not have dined at Chef Wang's flagship restaurant, where no one grudges spending the price of a racehorse on a dinner for two. Feature dishes include ragout of duck's tongues, and sea cucumber ovaries *aux baies de genièvre*. According to reviews, the food moves customers deeply: they weep and scribble notes on cocktail napkins sent back to the kitchen. Yet, ten thousand scribbled napkins cannot put into words the quality for which Chef Wang's art is famous—a quality almost beyond flavor, which no one can duplicate. A renowned food critic has written: *"Wang's cuisine, while delighting with its erudite and vivid fusion flavors, is most memorable for its eerie familiarity—as if this were the food our mothers had raised us on, on some distant, forgotten planet of common origin."* The only planet that interested Wang Kejia, though, was the Earth.

I have tasted Wang's cuisine. Twenty years ago, I shared a house with KJ and three other students at Boston University. He studied culinary arts and seemed pretty normal, but he had two gifts, one of them secret. KJ used to crave a Sichuan dish called *fuqi feipian*, which he said no one made right, and sometimes he cooked it, to the joy of us all. His food used to send a colossal sensation into every pore of my body. It was like eating a soul made of flesh, or—maybe that's what it was! I remember him as a wiry youth bent over the stove in his undershirt, cigarette in hand, stirring with wistful intensity. His other, secret gift came out suddenly one spring evening. After final exams we all went strolling along the Charles River, and as we crossed the footbridge near Harvard Square, KJ raced ahead and sprang high in the air. We gaped as he performed a somersault, landing with bent knees, symmetrically placed feet and heroic calves. Passers-by hooted and clapped. KJ tossed his bangs and said, "Did you believe a man can fly?"

Later, he told us that his grandfather, a martial artist, had been executed by the Red Guards. KJ practiced in his memory. Despite his ambition, spurred by his family's poverty, he was often very homesick. It's ironic that his customers, today, are the super-rich who have made Boston unaffordable for so many native Bostonians. But artists don't choose their clients. KJ's home is a taste, and his food tastes the way it does because the memory of starvation shapes his flavors. If any artist deserves success, it is my old housemate.

When KJ contacted me after two decades, I'd finished a year of chemotherapy and was in remission but broke. I'd sold everything I had to pay for the medical care that had turned me into a sort of ghost. I was counting the last of my pills that would need replacement somehow, without insurance coverage, using a checkered towel in whose squares I placed each pill. Then my iPhone, the only valuable thing not sold, lit up. I heard KJ's voice, a burnt-orange voice, all grit and allure. It was something to hear that voice in my empty apartment. We reminisced. I didn't mention cancer.

"You sound not so good," he said, "you sound kind of depressed. I'm offering you a chance to try something new. Why not? Take the chance!" He wanted to commission a series of tapestries depicting life's evolution. The tapestries would be displayed in the first luxury restaurant on the moon, which he'd named Giant Leap. He described a high-end venue for business leaders interested in the burgeoning lunar industries, a place more conducive to deal-making than the moon's dismal cafeterias. Why the evolution of life? Because décor must enhance the meaningful experience of his food. KJ hadn't been able to envision Giant Leap's interior scheme, until it hit him: what was the must-see sight on the moon?

I couldn't guess, so he told me: Earthrise. Every human on the moon, from miners to CEOs, liked to gather on the Earthrise Platform to see the home planet in space. This gave KJ an idea. The moon was like a high, high throne, the throne of humanity, with an empire laid at its feet. Now, he imagined Giant Leap as a regal, domed hall, where VIPs of all spacefaring nations would dine in style, surrounded   not by slick abstraction or space-themed kitsch—but by the unifying chronicle of the empire of life.

I was intrigued. And I liked KJ, always had. But if I hadn't been broke, I might have said that his dinosaur-munching-foliage idea was rather quaint. It sounded like the curtains of some eminent Victorian's bed. What was more, I had lost the strength to weave, probably forever. Still, I kept listening because his voice felt good. Then he told me about the Penrose system of time travel and his desire for authentic, *first-hand observations*. This was crazy, and a vision lit my heart. I gave a rough estimate for his project. Then, because time travel surely deserved hazard pay, I bargained for a bonus in the form of a Clayford-Gobelin Digital Tapestry Loom, the Silver Swan model.

Odds are you'll never see a Silver Swan. Weavers don't personally own them; a handful of companies and premier art schools do. A Silver Swan is like having a dozen studio assistants handling routine tasks, from warping to battening, in a single loom

so ingeniously programmed that it almost reads your mind. Even
weak, skin-and-bones me could weave wonders on a Silver Swan.
And I got it!

The next day, dozens of Fed Ex envelopes arrived at my door,
filled with an advance check, waivers galore, instructional mate-
rial, and a nondisclosure agreement. I signed everything. The Silver Swan arrived with two technicians who set it up, nonplussed
by my bare studio and its skeletal occupant. When they left, half
the room was loom.

How to describe it? It was a high-warp loom, vertical. Like
a steel waterfall over steel ledges that bore no clear relation to
familiar parts. Where was the apron rod? Were those beams? I
chose some yarns, followed the holo-instructor's demo for dressing the loom, carefully programmed a rosepath pattern with a
tabby weft, two-feet square, and powered on. Nothing happened.
I was resetting the instructor when a hiss, a hum, rushed through
the studio. The Silver Swan blurred. Then it stopped. There was
my finished piece. Another remote command, and the piece was
wound on an invisible cloth beam and detached. I examined it.
The selvedges were parallel, strictly parallel, as if they'd been la-
ser-guided. Wow, I owned a Silver Swan!

Doodling on it all day, I made samples of favorite weaves—
small diamonds, astrakhan, various inlays—and tapestry tech-
niques that would save me repetitive work. All perfect to the last
millimeter. Sometime in the wee hours I got a crude craving for
Rya knots, lots and lots of chunky knots in hot-colored cascades.
It was cold in my studio on an October night. My silver genie
blurred again, and the Rya piece materialized. Blurry-eyed, I
rolled the knots in my fingers. They were perfectly graded in size,
their tassels hung even as a ruler. The fuzzy warmth I'd hungered
for wasn't in the damn things. They were too perfect.

I looked around at the heaps of cloth the Silver Swan had
made for me, and wasn't satisfied. Well. Didn't magic always
have a catch?

Pondering the problem, I made steaming coffee and listened
to an ambulance siren winding through the blackness outside the

window. The Swan could be programmed for random changes to make its product less perfect. But programmed flaws never look like handmade, because the body's action isn't random.
I've taught weaving for years, and I read textile like print. Small
changes can show me if sore finger joints are affecting a student's
grip on the bobbin. They can show a personality, like the impul-
sive type who leaves bare bits of warp called lice—and if smart,
uses dyed warps to turn lice into color accents. I eyed my Silver
Swan, thinking.

Tapestry is about changes. Other kinds of cloth are woven by
throwing the weft clear across the warp. But with tapestry, you
weave only so far, then switch to a different weft, in a new bobbin,
and weave only so far before switching again. Dozens of bobbins
hang from your loom, clinking softly, awaiting their turn. Tapestry means thousands of changes that add up to a picture. Fin-
ishing one is a lot like when the clutter of daily life, the bits and
pieces, come together and you see, for a moment, like a snapshot,
what your life is.

I said to my artificially intelligent loom, "You're the answer
to my prayers, but that's why you don't get it." The Silver Swan
towered in the shadows and did exactly nothing, an off-duty angel. I'd have to partner with it somehow. You can imagine how I
spent the days and nights until, finally, like Death at the feast, a
new envelope arrived containing appointments and instructions
for my journey back through time.

Great Leap is in a restored brick factory near Kendall Square.
I arrived at 4:00 AM and hadn't eaten or drunk for twelve hours,
per orders. KJ was away on the moon, so we wouldn't meet, but
he'd texted good luck wishes, and an offer of dinner on my return. My, my. I texted back, "Fuqi feipian?" By the time I reached
Great Leap, the moon had sent emojis and a thumbs-up.

The floor above the restaurant is the lab. I was greeted by a
thirtyish woman in a lab coat, named Shivani, as thin and dark
as a cricket. She seemed to be having fun. Only doctors have
fun at that hour, and I said so. Laughing, she admitted that she
was an MD as well as a biologist, and ushered me into an oddly

proportioned room (the walk-in cooler). Four very young scientists gripped my hand, by turns, and spoke their names, which I forgot, distracted by their attitude toward Shivani. Their voices were lowered in respect, their words spare and precise. Their faces glowed. Plainly, Shivani was a power. Perched on an ergonomic stool, she dismissed her team, smiled at me, and gestured lightly.

"Welcome to the Penrose system. We'll apply the skinsuit right away so it can start feeding and hydrating you. Once it's on, you'll be very comfortable. Questions?" She cocked her head, and I confessed that I hadn't had time to read all the instructional materials, or, frankly, much of any of them. Shivani took my blood pressure, temperature and pulse, listened to my lungs, and gave me a wet swab to suck. It was like the nightmare of being back at the cancer clinic all over again.

"When do I start travelling?"

"You should be in the late Archean eon, which is around two thousand, eight hundred million years ago, probably by lunchtime."

The *ark eon*, I thought numbly. Two by two.

Shivani asked me to undress. When I did, she touched the port installed near my collarbone, and stepped back, frowning at my whole body. "You don't need to do this, you know? You can wait till you're stronger."

"I signed a contract."

Shivani folded her arms. "Look—if I tell Kejia that the subject is not ready, then the subject is not ready, and he must comply." She advised me to think it over for as long as I needed, and to pull a red cord when I'd decided.

I sat dangling my bare feet, seeing my checkered towel with pills in each square. The financial complications of backing out, now, were exhausting to consider. To my right hung those grey depths of exhaustion. To my left, an abyss of unknown danger. I thought of my Silver Swan, and KJ saying, "Take the chance!" And pulled the red cord.

Naked, depilated, I stood on a platform in a cylindrical chamber. Goggles protected my eyes; shields were taped to my ears and anus; my teeth clenched a plastic breathing tube. Shivani's voice came from a speaker.

"Ready for the application . . . now." Mist, chill and gluey, coated my skin and sealed my nose. Then air billowed from the floor, like a warm cushion into which I leaned. Three more applications to go.

Between times, as the layers dried, Shivani entertained me by explaining things. My skinsuit was polymer, impregnated with bacteria engineered to behave like a quantum computer: an electric signal sent them into multiple spacetimes. (She said "multiple spacetimes" like a routine detail, as I would mention rigid heddles.) But, she said, pausing to relish her punch line, the skinsuit bacteria were only *half* of the system.

She projected onto the chamber wall a blue human outline. "This is you, from today's examination. Watch." A green glow pulsed over the blue, thickening in the middle to a foggy coil. "The green, here, shows your body's bacteria, quite as many as your human cells. Large bodies, like you and me, can't exist in multiple spacetimes for more than a trillionth of a trillionth of a second. But bacteria are always time traveling and they can really hang around, because they're less than one Planck mass." (In the pulsing figure, I queasily recognized my intestines.) "At the signal, the skinsuit bugs enter the time travelling state and become quantum-entangled with your bugs. Basically, they're harnessed together. They pull you through time like two dog teams pulling a sled. We've designed the skinsuit bugs to seek mineral isotopes that are present only in the time we're aiming for."

I made a noise and removed my mouth tube. "Could you turn off this projection? It's . . . visceral."

The blue-green ghost switched off and the doctor added, sympathetically, "We don't think of ourselves like this, I know. We think we're individuals, there's just one soul per body, and that's kind of sacred to our idea of self. But we are both one and many. Working with the Penrose system, I'm used to thinking of myself"— Shivani paused, and I could almost see how she gestured at her energetic, lab-coated body—"as an ecosystem for billions of tiny creatures, that calls itself 'me'. You'll be a time traveler, but it's not really about you. It's about bacteria going all over spacetime for their own reasons, carrying you along."

Not quite following, I sat up abruptly in the air cushion and fell over. "Shivani! How do I get back?" KJ had scrupulously mentioned the lost Canadian. "What about the Canadian?" I blurted, trying to right myself.

"That . . . was before my time. Though I looked into the case, and it seems the Canadian paid my predecessor—a lot—to create a one-way ticket. Scientific knowledge was not prioritized." Her pause was graphically withering. "No worries. You're our first human subject, but robots and rats have made the round trip reliably. The system is robust. After twenty-four hours, the travelling state collapses and you automatically return home. How are you feeling?"

Seated again on my air pillow, I felt oddly as if I'd eaten breakfast. And air came through my nose! That meant the skinsuit was running: it would nourish and hydrate me, provide oxygen, recycle waste, and bring me home. I was asked only to keep my mouth closed, especially outdoors, unless I had to consume extra supplies. I surveyed the wondrous coating in which I resembled a stale gummy bear, or a berserk condom.

"I thought—I don't know, I'd be given a rifle against dinosaurs, and enjoy fresh air and hiking."

"You're going to the Archean eon," Shivani repeated. "The air will be mostly methane and nitrogen. There will be no wild animals. There will be no animals at all, with one exception."

"Which is—?"

"You," Shivani clarified.

My gummy hands covered my gummy breast, and to say I felt alone would be to say that I felt at all.

To fill the expanding silence, Shivani gently, and as it were intimately (given that I was naked and committed), shared the philosophy behind the Penrose system. It was about the uncertainty principle's being untrue. That surprised me. Before cancer, you know, I'd enjoyed my Sunday paper. Once, I'd seen a cartoon of a cat with just half its fur on end. It was about the famous thought experiment in which a cat, in a sealed box, had a fifty-fifty chance of being alive or dead until a scientist measured the speed of a particle. The experimenter influences the experiment, and whatnot. As I recalled this to the good doctor (or whatever sort of doctor she was), I broke out in gummy goosebumps. I was being sent into multiple spacetimes, multiple probabilities. *I* was the imaginary cat.

"No, no," Shivani rejoined, with a sweetness not quite laughter, "Schrodinger's cat is a fallacy, Penrose proved that."

"But . . . isn't the cat's life uncertain until a scientist measures the particle?"

"We don't think so," Shivani declared, using the royal *we* of global science. "Human observations are not the cat's problem, or the universe's problem—why should they be? Why should a primate species with a brief, rather nasty history be so important? Honestly, can you imagine the structure of reality depending on the actions of anyone you know?" She let this sink in, and concluded briskly, "No worries. Nature herself will bring you back."

With that, they sent me.

*   *   *

I was stumbling in strong gusts of wind. I saw the silver tent hovering over the metal stump called the buoy, labelled in red print, "DANGER!!! DO NOT ATTEMPT TO MOVE, ALTER OR DESTROY BUOY." Per instructions, I pulled the tent's fluttering tab. The tent sank to the height of a step, a flap unpeeled, and I climbed inside to inspect the supplies and gadgets strapped to its taut walls and floor. Shivani had briefed me thoroughly between skinsuit applications, and all was as she had described. That was something. Then I gathered myself in lotus pose before the open flap, and the view.

A tea-colored mist was blowing over a stony slope descending to the sea. The surf was fast and violent. At noon, the light was thin as dawn; I had gone back so far that the sun was immature. Trying to sniff the sea, I inhaled the smell of new skinsuit. I had water in my catch-tube, and a comfortable temperature. I dressed in camo—absurdly, since neither plants nor animals existed yet—strapped on equipment, and jumped out of the tent. Gravel crunched.

Behind me rose a wide arc of cliffs, several hundred feet high and flat-topped, like an open accordion of gray rock. I was standing in a semicircular fjord, wondering how far the tide would enter. Not far, judging from the unstained buoy. Hunching into the wind, I walked to the shore.

The scenery was poorly lit and noisy. The wind moaned, the sea crashed, and besides the surf's rumble, I felt in my bones a chthonic mutter that would have made a dog whine. To feel what the ground was doing, I squatted and scooped up pebbles—a grayscale of granite, a salt-and-pepper scattering of quartz and basalt. Something about them bugged me, though they would have been at home on any north Atlantic beach. I sieved them through my fingers, sensing wrongness. Maybe it was the lost feeling carried on the brownish mist. No map would ever name this beach, these cliffs, drifting across time toward the formation of Africa or Australia, or, possibly, headed down to the ocean floor, into the maw of a subduction vent to be crushed and vaporized in the earth's gut. A strange place, this. I might as well trudge along the floor of a dream. These thoughts were uneasy enough, but they didn't explain the wrongness, either.

Near the shoreline, where foam charged my river shoes, tearing at pebbles underfoot, I watched for a while to get my bearings. The noon sky had a yellow cast. The sea made a beige tumult in the shallows, where breakers toppled. Trying to figure how the tide ran, I noticed dark streaks about a mile out; on a sandier beach, I would have thought them sand-bars. Whales they were not. Coral reefs, not. Past the streaks, in the distance where the modern sea keeps its profound blues, the Archean ocean looked like it had been used to wash dirty floors. Well, it had. I knew a little about the sea from a project I'd done, weaving marine plastic. Nothing lived yet in those waters to filter out the grubby dust of creation, and sequester the carbon, and make things pleasant.

About three miles out, shapes studded the view like snowless copies of Mount Fuji. I blinked hard, since I couldn't rub my eyes through goggles. Was the haze darker there? Those must be volcanic islands, which could explain the subaudible tremor in the ground, and the rushing foam's tropical warmth. Under my shoes, Earth was still mostly liquid fire.

Then I understood what was wrong with the beach. While I'd been orienting myself, the tide had been ebbing. I followed the waterline to a rim of black mud, walking along it. Once, I looked back at the only footprints for the next billion years. I watched the foam scour them away. Every beach I'd walked on had shone like this as the sea licked it, and gone dull as the sea drained back. But no sand-flies were zigzagging in my face. Some way into the shallows, a car-sized rock was emerging from a seawater churn. I waded in.

My strength was a surprise, the gift of the skinsuit; balancing against the knock of the waves, I advanced steadily, spitting out toxic-tasting spray that got between my lips. Before long, I pulled myself by handholds around the giant rock. It was wildly pitted, as if a dragon brood had wormed its way out of the iron-hard stone. And in all those sheltering pits, I saw no hint of slime. No green or red streaks, no rusty moss, no sea-fleas. No encrusted barnacles. No seaweed clinging as it swayed in rhythm. No snails. No secretive little mussels. No guano, obviously . . .

In every twisted pit through the rock there was only the black of space.

A wave threw me like a tumbler of stinging pebbles. No jellyfish. I half-swam, half-slopped back in a hurry, pelted by underwater stones. On land again, I caught my breath and gazed ahead, where the long strand of mud shone like polished onyx, unmarred by so much as a bubble, or a breathing dimple.

The wrongness, which words can't touch, was really something. Like being locked after hours in a poisoned and barren construction site.

After rubbernecking, I had jobs to do: visual information to gather for the tapestry project, and some fieldwork for the lab. The field kit on my hip included an ARMV—'augmented reality microscopic view'—a headset that worked as a digital microscope and vidcam in one. I had walked nearly to one end of the fjord, where granite cliffs plunged into the surf. Suddenly, I heard loud humming at my back and whirled to face—out of the hazy, yellow sky—the hover-tent! I stared at the silver pod humming in midair like a hornet. Recalling that it was programmed to escort me beyond a set perimeter, I put my palms together and bowed, because fine tools demand respect. Thereafter it glided along with a pensive murmur.

Nothing else surprised me until I came across a herd of small hippos. That weren't hippos. I kept having to wrestle with such illusions—gulls that weren't, crabs that weren't. But this new sight matched the lab's description. Taking a deep breath, I waded out among the boulders resting in low water. They were wrinkled mounds, soft-looking, like petrified sofa cushions. Their color was soft too, mottled with subtle tints like Irish heather yarn. I touched one, and wow! It was sticky.

"Whoohoo!" I yelled and waved my arms at the tent. "Yay!" The world's first words were a hoarse cheer. I sloshed from boulder to boulder, patting their sides sticky with organic life. Honestly, I could have hugged them.

Instead, I unfolded the ARMV. Using it first as a hand-held vidcam, I scanned the boulders. Shivani had said that they were made of bacterial films laminated with dust. As the bugs multiplied, new films covered the old, and the boulders grew, part life, part dust. They were called stromatolites. Of all the recorded forms of life, these were the earliest, resting around me lapped by wrist-high waves in pale sunlight. From dust, I thought, from dust. Hallelujah.

Choosing a flattish stromatolite close to shore, I knelt in the shallows. Fortunately, the ARMV's complicated settings had been fixed in advance; I only had to put my head inside and watch the stromatolite. I raised the headset, and baulked. From my belly came a warning not to put on the headset. I re-checked the shoulder rests, re-tightened the rear strap, and tried again. And couldn't. Instinct cried that to cover my eyes, alone in this strange place, was folly. Yet the whole planet wasn't as dangerous, for a woman alone, as my neighborhood off Massachusetts Avenue. What was the threat? Psycho stromatolites?

Holding the headset under one arm, I stood and did a sloppy jig, trying to shake off fear, and noticed a large shadow, criss-crossed by transparent ripples, cast by the floating hover-tent nearby.

"Tent!" I called. It was at my shoulder, front flap unpeeling. "This is only a test," I said. "Away, please." The tent glided a few feet off. I resumed my watery seat beside the stromatolite. Still the headset felt like a guillotine.

Shivani had briefed me on the ARMV. The view would magnify the bacteria and intensify their natural colors, an aid to scientists studying the record. The view's margins, crammed with data and animated graphs, were also for the scientists. My job was just to look. A robot could do it. But KJ needed an artist, Shivani and her team needed a human subject . . . and I had pulled a red cord. Breathing fast, I settled the ARMV over my head. Everything went black.

Then under my gaze stretched a swathe of dewy, pink bumps filled with subtle motion, a sort of kinetic twinkling. Like a sunrise, the pink held purple and orange streaks that came and went, clouded over by the pink bumps or given space to reappear. The colors were alive, lush and fresh. Eastward, the pink thickened into a rosy ridge, beyond which spread a different species ten times as large. These big neighbors were green spheres, their clear membranes dotted with fuzz. They had, I must say, an air. They didn't live in crowds, but in chrysanthemum-shaped knots of trailing strands. Within the strands, the motion of each sphere was like the sentient oscillation of a bee. As I watched, some strands divided, others shrank, and single spheres unmoored and collected followers, bright as sunned leaves. Over the whole scene hung a bewitching harmony. I watched for a long time. These were biofilms, the stuff you wipe off a sink, or skim off a pool, but I was filled with reverence. Raw life in its rainbow snakeskin gliding from the void.

I noticed a pattern. Steadily, the green zone was inching into the pink. That was interesting. Something was up. I scanned the data scrolling in the margins; as my focus moved, graphs changed; mostly cryptic, but I knew the symbol for oxygen. O_2's graph spiked over the green, and fell elsewhere. How thrilling—like a tiny forest, my green spheres were exhaling oxygen! Here was Eden, the earliest photosynthesis. Which meant, yes, the green zone used water, and was expanding as the tide crept up.

I noticed another pattern: one sphere, a pair, a few would gather, and after a mysterious pause, a whole colony would bloom. The uneven rhythm, long-pause-and-bloom, was maddeningly familiar until it came to me—*the same rhythm as drawing yarn through warp to make a tapestry stitch.* Now I saw how to design KJ's tapestry, but it would demand something I'd always avoided. Yeah. Gazing again at the ridge between species, I saw that the green zone was now, unaccountably, shrinking. Puzzled, I removed the ARMV, blinked away retinal ghosts, and collapsed the device. I stood stiffly, trousers caked with silt.

Twilight had come, the brownish pallor of a fall evening, and the wind had sunken. Around me, stromatolites sat exposed on the mud. Far away, on the horizon, each volcano stuck a fiery fang into low-hung clouds that were amassing swiftly, heads hidden except where trees of lightning struck across their vague breadth. Lightning glinted off the ocean, which had retreated so far that the big rock I'd swum around earlier was exposed, about a quarter mile off. Curious, I walked toward it until the mud made progress tiresome. Within a stone's throw of the giant boulder, I saw that it tilted steeply, half buried, as if rammed aslant into the sea floor. Beyond, in the dusk, some large formations were discernible, and I recalled dark streaks in the sea at those positions. A lifetime's weaving has taught me to remember positions. I made out mounded shapes, protruding from the mud like worn molars, in a broken arc. I knew that arc. I'd felt it at my back all day: the curve of the fjord's cliffs. It was mirrored in those undersea mounds. The two arcs, cliffs and mounds, described a ring around the big, half-buried rock. My, my.

I was standing in an impact crater, where space-iron had dropped and splashed up a circle of cliffs, in a long-ago eon of liquid rock. For an instant, the Archean by contrast felt normal—for about a trillionth of a trillionth of a second.

The landscape became easier to see. I thought my eyes were acclimating to darkness, until—as if a police car had driven up behind me—a floodlight swept past my feet. Light threw a long shadow of a creature like myself on the rippled mud. Turning around, I saw the cliffs illuminated. And from end to end of the clifftops, across their entire summit, was parked the glowing dome of a spaceship.

I couldn't budge. The thing was out of proportion to human thought. I watched as the dome shouldered—it was moving!—by degrees gently up the night sky; and it was the moon.

Not my moon, with the twinkle of Huawei Station in its cheek. Not my dead parents' proud American moon. Not KJ's moon. Rimmed craters, spidery ridges, were near enough to finger. No one knew this young moon, torn from its home, still lingering close over Earth. Unconsciously, because it seemed to be toppling, I fended off the moon, overbalanced, and fell on my ass in the mud.

The only animal on the planet felt embarrassed.

I stood, but fell again. On hands and knees, I saw pewter-colored mud all around me cracking apart like clay. The mutter in the ground rose to a sky-high roar. Shit, I thought: earthquake.

Gaining my feet in a string of pratfalls, I sprinted toward the cliffs, yelling for the tent. I couldn't hear my own voice. But the tent heard. I ran headlong to meet its airborne silver form, and in the corner of my eye saw—not volcanoes' earthshaking glow—but a high wall of moonlit cliffs *behind me*. The sight spun me into such a terror, I didn't know which direction I was running in. Then those new cliffs out of nowhere betrayed their glassy, oncoming swell, their summits sagging in huge explosions of foam.

Screaming for the tent, I lunged for its open flap, and struggled to enter as the tent accelerated upwards. Trying to kick my
way in, my feet struck a claw of high-rise ocean. The tsunami
raced inches below with the sight and sound of universal collapse.
I was nearly inside when a thunderclap blew the air apart, and
I fell.

*   *   *

The mind works a moment after the heart stops, a prey animal's last thought in death's jaws. A yellow flame appears
and swells to the size of a cave. In the cave stands a sloe-eyed
horse, with ears wisely pricked. Astride the horse is a rider,
barefoot, in loose trousers. Firelight and shadow play over
his bare chest, sweating red drops as if he's ridden in a rain
of blood. He and the horse are a single animal, trousers and
flanks bloodied. He has come through such sights that his eyes
have no whites at all.

*   *   *

My eyes were closed. I called out, to tell the lab I was awake. Let
them get me out of the tent, whose slippery fabric I felt, and
the skinsuit. I needed a hot bath, something for headache, coffee and toast, my clothes, and a ride home to my Silver Swan. I
called again, and my eyes opened. My ears popped and heard
the sound of surf.

There was no point in tears. I'd survived an earthquake, a
tsunami, and a lightning strike that had thrown me headfirst into
the tent instead of the sea. That was good. Good enough is the
jackpot, as I used to tell the hurrying nurses at the cancer clinic.

I sat up unsteadily, unclipped my muddied pack, and found the
ARMV in one piece. Memories were difficult to sort. I lacked any
sense of elapsed time since losing consciousness, although there
was a nagging notion of some experience—besides stromalites,
moon, and tsunami—that had been important. Whatever it was,

it nagged like a traveling itch, with the effect of making me worry that somehow, in my sleep, I'd bungled the automatic return trip. I hunted through the tent's pockets for the timer, which showed five hours left to go in the Archean. No, I hadn't missed the return! Limp with relief, I gave up on the whatever-it-was, and set about unpacking some nutrient pills and skinsuit cleanser wipes. A comprehensive stretch restored circulation to my muscles; afterwards, a refreshing nap. One change of clothes was mercifully available. At last, I went outside.

The first thing to meet my eyes was the buoy. Astonished, I bent to examine it. The sleek metal stump of yesterday looked like it had been blowtorched long enough to melt its corners, then peppered with shot and attacked with files and sanders. The red print was gone; by all signs, long gone. It was not the same buoy. Yet there was only one buoy. Shivani had said so.

I whistled in awe, but stopped mid-whistle to rub a polymerized finger over a scratched, discolored area. My finger stained. I couldn't smell it, so, ignoring Shivani's orders, I licked it and tasted iron. The buoy was rusted! But the Archean air didn't hold enough oxygen to rust iron. I tasted my finger again, and stood gaping in the light—the clear, full morning light—that shone on the broken brows of the low cliffs. They were a ruin, half the height they'd been yesterday. Above them arched a vacant, radiant, blue sky.

Well, I thought, the tsunami must have mangled the buoy, cut cliffs in half, and changed the atmosphere in one night. It was a beautiful morning, with daffodil sunlight and a playful breeze. I walked down to the shore, where hundreds upon hundreds of hippos—that weren't—sunbathed back to back in the sparkling shallows. Over their wrinkled hides shimmered tints in oily patterns. The stromatolites had colonized the entire stretch of shallows out to the drop-off into the sea. And the sea was blue, embracing the blue sky. I could have walked on the stromatolites for a mile toward the blue water. The trouble with this scene was that it could not be real.

I was stunned like a clobbered cow.

A lifetime of weaving makes logic second only to patience. Necessities—such as having to re-loop, by hand, two hundred heddle loops to fix an error—inculcate the habit of analysis under stress. #1: I'd traveled to another time where the lab never meant me to go. #2: I was unconscious and dreaming. #3: The whatever-it-was that I found impossible to remember was my own death.

Weeping into the goggles despite myself, I unpacked the ARMV and took hand-held measurements in case #1 was true. Lo and behold. There was more oxygen in the air, not enough for my poor nose, but sufficient to rust iron. That was interesting. My green spheres had exhaled oxygen, and here must be the sum of their tiny sighs, millions of years on. My, my. As for #2, if I were dreaming about atmospheric oxygen, why the hell hadn't I made a career in science? With better health benefits. I'm almost never angry, but suddenly I shook with rage. As for #3! If KJ had called me because I was the best artist he could get without a family to sue for wrongful death—then he'd made a smart move, hadn't he.

The sun was climbing. I stripped, threw my clothes, shoes, and ARMV on the beach, and ran barefoot over the sleepy, sticky hippos until I fell into the sea, and dived downward into depths where the sun's rays wheeled. Down there, I saw the stromatolite towers, the bottomless towers, branching like candelabra through fathoms of still light. Nothing swam, nothing would swim for half a billion years, except me, trailing bubbles like a plumbline. The only animal in the world spiraled around the Atlantis of the first ancestors. My tiny shadow whisked across the silent city walls. Nothing was hunting, nothing fled, nothing lurked in wait. The myths were all untold.

The living tapestry whose work-rhythm I'd felt now unfolded to my sight its grand scene: life had cleared and cleaned the sky and ocean, and made them habitable. Animals would follow, but the original empire did not dream of us, only of peace. I stretched out my hands and hit a metal wall.

*   *   *

I stayed in the lab for a week, recovering. When I returned home, everything I touched was lit from within and fragile as paper. My red coffee mug, the threadbare bathroom towel. My neighborhood, too. Ordinary places like the CVS beside the subway entrance and the Spanish Haitian grocery were paper lantern facades, glowing with a tender intention to be real. I caught up with my social media acquaintanceship and answered some invitations to teach workshops, but people also seemed unreal. The one solid thing was my Silver Swan.

I worked steadily, absorbed in a technique I'd always disdained. But now that I'd been where I'd been and done what I'd done, and returned to find reality not quite itself—what was the harm? Everything had changed and gone on changing since I'd taken KJ's dare and pulled that red cord in the lab. Weaving like this was just another change. . . . I loved this new work that I was doing, for in it alone, I was truly home. Sometimes as I wove, a window in time opened and I'd see KJ standing at the stove, cigarette in one hand, with the other stirring a fresh-cooked dish. I'd see the homesick man I'd known all those years ago. As we worked in tandem, weaving and cooking, I'd feel that I had waited a long time to share with him this making of home by hand, through the vanishing hours. I'd stopped wondering whether he'd hired me because I had no relatives to bring lawsuits, or because he'd liked my work best, or for some other reason. What had happened between him and me now felt as mysterious and meaningful as the fluid patterns I'd seen taking shape on the stromatolite.

The only interruptions I endured were checkups—free, for the Penrose lab's human subject. Though I was still in remission, my red blood cell count was borderline. Shivani insisted that I eat lean red meat and become a vegan later. I knew she was right, but food no longer looked like proper objects to put in my mouth. Though I'd managed to get through chemo with a fair appetite, I now subsisted on Ensure and apple sauce, along with the meds that Shivani, glowering, prescribed. Whether at her instigation or not, it wasn't long before KJ kept his word and invited me to dinner at Great Leap.

Our foursome—KJ, Shivani, her husband Raju, and me—
shared an alcove with a midcentury look: cream walls half-pan-
eled in oak, black crane lamps at odd angles. KJ joked about
being an executive chef who hardly set foot in a kitchen anymore,
although, he promised, some of the dishes we'd taste tonight were
his handiwork. We admired the industrial glass tabletop, and the
dinner service—was it formica? No, a porcelain imitation.

Raju raised a saucer to his ear and tapped on it. "Aha," he
confirmed, "the ring of truth."

His wife sparkled, smoothing her iridescent hair, and regaled
us with new discoveries from the ARMV, which she had retrieved
via robot, thanks to the damaged but still functional buoy. I expressed regret for losing the headset, and Shivani said that I was a
hero. Wine and tea were poured. At first, our host hadn't known
me—a bald head poking from a woven red wrap that served as
evening dress. I looked like a Buddhist monk dropped in a wine
vat. As the *amuse-bouches* were served, KJ kept glancing at me with
a kind of wounded respect. I smiled, touching nothing. The cel-
ebrated entrees went round, Chinese style, and I spooned food
onto my plate, where it grew cold. Shivani noticed, frowning, but
refrained from medical comment.

I was on my own, therefore, when KJ dipped a morsel of rice
in sauce and held it on the end of his chopsticks, in my face.

Irresistibly, everything—conversation, laughter, even the rising steam—stopped. I opened my lips, couldn't say a word, and
shut my eyes. Bite by bite, he fed me *fuqi feipian*. A colossal sensation flooded out of memory into my body's every pore, releasing
tears of a special flavor.

"Crying is the Great Leap thing," Shivani assured Raju.

"It's the Great Leap thing," KJ echoed smugly. I nodded, blowing my nose and marveling.

"I dreamed about you, KJ—back there. You were on a horse,
and you were sweating drops of blood, and the horse was, too."

His handsome brows rose. "*Hanxuema*. Blood-sweating horse.
That was a famous breed in China, highly valued, but I think
your dream means something else."

With one voice we asked, what?

"You need to eat," he told me.

*   *   *

After dinner, we received simultaneous alerts about the tide surge, and any pleasure in lingering vanished. Raju offered me a ride, but KJ—thanking everyone for the pleasure, etc.—escorted me home in his chauffeured Porsche. I sat with him in back, wrapping myself tighter. We watched the river, wind-whipped and swollen, sprayed through a mess of honking cars, stalled buses, mounted police, and pedestrians issuing out of the filthy waterfall of the subway station. Between radio announcements, the chauffeur grumbled.

"Global wahming, just like they been tellin' us for years. Now the Chahles is backin' up into the main ahteries." His broad, stable neck swiveled side to side.

"Huh," KJ agreed. "On the moon, we can use this water." He wasn't joking.

"You can have it." The Porsche churned up onto the sidewalk by my apartment building. KJ got out, stood in the river, and helped me—red wrap, tote bag and all—onto my front step. In the wind, we called good-bye and I stood waving, tasting the sea, cheered to be waving in wet gusts so much like the lonely Archean.

Upstairs in my studio, I planned to work through the night. I switched on all the lights and the radio, low volume, and powered the Silver Swan. It projected a holographic cartoon behind the incomplete tapestry. I climbed on my stool and surveyed the life-size cartoon through the bare warp threads. From the woven section bobbins hung, skeins of lime, rose, and a dozen other yarns. Should I set the program running, or do hand-stitching first? Stretching my palms out, fingers laced, I felt energy leaping to be spent. Then the lights blinked. The room was dark. WBUR began playing "The Lights Went Out in Massachusetts," like an annoying friend repeating a once-successful joke;

and a reporter—in a well-lit studio, probably—began chatting about the blackout and our regional predicaments.

Sighing, I went to the closet and fumbled for the Coleman lanterns. Placed at optimum distance, on table and stovetop, they shone twinned in the black window. I pressed my nose to the pane and looked into the street, a canal of ink. Across the way, in another building's windows, restless light—tiny candles, hunting flashlights, beaming smartphones—showed my neighbors in the common darkness. Dispirited, turning back to my dead loom, I gave a shout. As I held the lantern up, pink bumps spread and flowed; purple and orange lines winked; green bubbles streamed and flowed. My tapestry was alive! The illusion was perfect now, heightened by shadows. I'd avoided this technique of optical blending, using colors to trick the brain into seeing change, because it had always seemed like cheating. Well, I thought, cheating or not, that looks pretty good. And I won't be the first woman to do handiwork by lamplight.

I got back on my stool, picked a bobbin, and worked on the soumak stitches defining the ridge between species, remembering how I'd dived down among the stromatolite towers. Slowly weaving my stitch and pulling it taut, I remembered how I'd wanted to un-become the animal I was, that feared death, fought death, and ate death. How different from the peaceful comity of bacteria whose exhalations made the sky blue, who flowed together across spacetime. I wanted to share my memory of the Atlantis of the first ancestors, but in recreating it I would also share this body, these hands, that had borne the violence of wind and sea, earthquake and lightning, cancer, grief, and economics.

I had made some good progress when a noise scared me. *Rat-tat!* Like a séance! *Rat-tat!* It came from my bedroom, a former closet with one window. Four stories up, no fire escape. Hairs rose on my spine. I crept into the bedroom, listening; rushed to lift the sash, and leaned out.

A few feet away, braced against a drainpipe and clinging to it by one arm, KJ waved urgently at me. I asked what the hell he was doing.

I saw his teeth shine. In a voice low enough to be heard without waking neighbors, he crooned, "I left my cigarettes in your handbag."

Incredulous, I went to look in my WBUR canvas tote, and found a pack of Dunhill's.

"It's here," I murmured out the window. "I'll leave it at the restaurant." But he wanted a smoke now. Could he come in? I told him to get back down, it was dangerous. He swung a little, like a mix of Fred Astaire and a cyclops moth.

"Why can't I come in?" cajoled the burnt-orange voice.

"It's three in the morning."

"Awh! Throw me my cigarettes."

Holding my breath, I tossed the pack, which he caught one-handed. Loosening fingers from the drainpipe, he extracted a cigarette, a lighter; and an ember gilded his face.

"What about tomorrow?" he asked, blowing smoke and laughing silently. I hadn't thought about tomorrow, in a general way, for a long time. My, my. An instinct that was pure animal but not fear rejoiced me, although it seemed that we were more or less doomed, all of us. Yet I knew that everything changes, changes utterly, even doom changes.

"We'll see tomorrow, Kejia."

We smiled at each other across the dark.

THE WEREDOG

Yesterday, as sun streamed into the bathtub, I was drying myself
and noticed a shadow on the tub's side that looked like a dog. As
I stepped out, the dog-shadow slid off the tub and onto the white
shag rug. When I lifted one foot, it raised its forepaw. When I lifted the other foot, it raised its other paw. I looked around the tiny
bathroom, an eaves furnished with a meagre sink on a pedestal,
a toilet, a brass hook. Nothing threw an odd shadow except me.
When I jumped, with both feet, my shadow shook itself dry. Ever
since, I've been attached to a black German shepherd in two
dimensions.

*

If I could only get out. From a window in Aunt's office, where
I sleep, I gaze through transparent fangs into the snowbound
yard below. My shadow lies on the cot, on its back, two hind-
paws stretched up the wall like black asparagus. As I descend the
curved stairway to the first floor, my shadow fans into a whole
pack of dogs, jostling playfully.

*

I eat at the glass kitchen table, my dog-shadow crouched beneath, by the chrome legs. When I hold out a bagel piece, it
snaps up the bit of bagel-shadow. A pet, nice. The newspaper
is weeks old; no mail comes through the front door slot, locat-
ed halfway down a snowdrift. Polar sunlight glares through
Aunt's jade plants in their window above the sink, a jungle
that she has nurtured through forty years of Uncle's typical
acoustics.

"HOOOW MANY TIMES HAVE I TOLD YOU THAT *I HAAAAATE CAULIIIIFLOOOWWER!!!!!*" Thus Uncle, at table. Aunt chucks the offending vegetable in the trash, fetches him some bread, and stares into her plants. Later, a current of feeling runs between the old couple's eyes, her bluets, his blue ice.

Now she's waiting in a hospital hotel, with medical staff telling her they're not to blame, and paying for her room until the weather abates enough to bring Uncle home.

*

One day, as Aunt was ironing in the basement, Uncle charged down the stairs and, complaining loudly, threw her into the wall head-first. For a week she felt disoriented and could hardly find her way from room to room; when she drove to see a psychiatrist, she got lost. She was late. The psychiatrist told her coldly that he did not see unpunctual patients. She said she was afraid her husband would kill her. The shrink stressed that her lack of commitment, implied by unpunctuality, was not something he brooked in his patients. Aunt went home and started collecting jade plants.

Uncle never hurt her body again, and his resolve fueled his irritable shouting. God knows what his decibels did to the pipes. This house has always had leaks, stopped toilets, showers with shuddering water pressure.

*

While I water the philodendrons on the second floor, my shadow skulks behind me; I think he's male, blocky-muzzled. Either I'm turning into a pooch-mad spinster, or else it's the influence of Grandfather, whose eyes were even icier than Uncle's, and who used to shake his head over the news that I was dating someone.

"Men are dogs," he'd warn me. "You earn a good living. What do you need it for?" The wonder in his voice was sincere.

*

That pair, Uncle's father and mother—once, I saw them in this very living room with its glum fern that I'm watering, its Tudoresque oak beams and carved heraldic seal over the hearth. (Whatever this clubbish room wants, it isn't Aunt's little candy-hued Mexican skulls lined up on the mantelpiece). So, here they sat. Grandfather looked most of his life like a sea-lashed cliff; he did heavy labor daily to put us in the middle class, and by that point, the cliff was half-collapsed. His hands were like boulders, and in one of them a coffee cup was buried. Grandmother had always resembled a small hill that you'd lie on in summer. Now she, whose days were spent on her feet working, resembled a small hill at dusk. Her hands were in her lap, her head was bent. Maybe she was crocheting an afghan, I wish I knew. Grandfather wanted her to look at him, and she wouldn't.

"Bessie," he teased, "the galaxies are calling to each other across the stars, and they're calling, 'Bessie!'"

Grandmother's head was bent. But she cocked one eye. "When I'm dead," she replied, "you'll be calling me."

I don't forget the monotone in which she delivered this curse, nor its eventual and precise effect.

*

Stupendous, this storm. WiFi is dead in our metropolitan area. On TV, on radio, they say that governors in nine states have restricted public transportation to all but medical and other essential workers. I'm lucky to be house-sitting in this safe shelter, though the polar wind fumbles with the house. The power's probably out in my apartment, but I emptied the fridge before coming here (half a pizza and milk, easy). Good thing I'm local, unlike Aunt's children whom the storm has grounded in far-flung cities. Sometimes I hear, far off, a car's spasmodic cough. At night, I turn a light on to keep my guard dog with me.

*

God! The landline rings—a special phone for the hard of hearing—at terrifying volume! Aunt is calling to check on the plants. All good, I say, and ask after Uncle.

"His life signs are stable but he hasn't woken up. After ten days, they say his brain could go."

"It won't be ten days," I declare, just as I told Uncle, leaving for the airport, that he'd get through his spine operation with flying colors. I said he'd come home walking upright. To change the subject, I describe my shadow. Wonderful Aunt doesn't waste breath on the obvious, but instead asks, why a dog?

"I tried changing my clothes, but it's always a dog. The only time I don't see it is in the dark."

"That's interesting." Her tone makes me grasp how dull, how morbidly dull, it is to sit in doctors' offices having your questions half-answered and your husband half alive. "Did you look on the Internet?"

"WiFi's dead. I'm actually getting work done." (I'm an accountant for a lab that breeds patented fruit flies. The main excitement in my job is when our proprietary genetics escape and zigzag through the halls, frantic for all they're missing.) In Aunt's pause, I hear the pretty engine of her imagination turning over.

"Why don't you look around my bookshelves? I have some good books up there." Aunt is wistful.

*

Steep stairs, shag-carpeted in mustard green, and at the top I'm finally above the world, in Aunt's office. My feet just fit between the cot, lovingly dressed for me in floral quilts, and a desk piled with brittle notepads whose leaves fall if touched. Taped to the wall is a printed-out email—*It is a Great idea. . . . Good Luck!*—curling into itself.

Aunt built her office after the kids were grown. Here, she designed a stylish novelty brooch. When pressed, it activated a hologram of a flapping bat accompanied by a synthesized chorus singing, *Don't drive me batty!*—or the equivalent in other languages from bat-wary cultures. The BattyBrooch enjoyed a nano-vogue among Japanese businesswomen looking for civil ways to avert *sekuhara*. On the strength of it, Aunt became a consultant. Until the crash of 2008, she travelled widely, teaching corporate employees to search their life-experiences for marketable ideas. With her earnings, she built the attic office, where I hear wind in the high boughs of the hemlocks.

*

As an accountant, I help the scientists, I help truth. Okay, what I investigate may not be the balance of the cosmos, but I know how to calculate so that a researcher's dream and its real-life obligations reach a total we can all live with. That's surely something. Everyone knows who I am and what I stand for. When questions arise, the National Institute of Health could strip me to the skin and find nothing on me but the honest truth. That's what "accountable" means: someone like me, counting numbers that I have verified as correct. There are dishonest truths, too; but the honest truths are told by numbers.

*

Aunt and I differ about the worth of dreams. Since I was young and undercapitalized, Aunt has been telling me that dreams can reveal the secret invention lurking in my inmost heart, the one worth a lot to people willing to pay. Lucid dreaming helped several of her clients become entrepreneurs.

"What are your dreams telling you?" she'll ask.

"I saw a row of dancers," I told her once, during a long phone chat. "They were chanting." The words, Aunt probed—did I remember their words?

I did. "They were chanting,
I do not want your hands
on the knobs
at the center of the Earth!"

I heard Uncle roaring something about an electric bill. I held
the phone away from my ear, but not far enough to miss Aunt's
exasperated cry, "Arnold! *You have corrected me!*" Then she resumed
our conversation. "Maybe your dream is about inventing a new
kind of knob. You should concentrate on knobs before you fall
asleep."

*

The cold today is all the TV news. Nothing like it since 1816.
Worse than 1816. Fleets of jetliners grounded. Jeeps racing
across Lake Erie. Icicles the height of office towers. Scores of
homeless people sarcophagized in snow. Puffs of wind killing
on contact. I put a muffin in the toaster oven and watch its
wires redden, for comfort. My dog-shadow waits, blurry tongue
lolling.

If Uncle were here, I'd skip lunch, because he likes to cross-ex-
amine at the table. Before retiring from his law practice, Uncle
terrified witnesses—not just any witnesses, but tough guys who
worked on racetracks and in mafia fronts. His questioning always
ended with a triple snarl—"Haa? *Haa? HAA?*" Then he'd turn
coolly to his notes. In the case of Aunt, his children, or me, he
turns instead to the newspaper, having wrung the facts from us,
and tells Aunt to put another thick slice of rye—by which he
means the following: less than two inches, but more than the
crummy half-inch she keeps giving him, which FALLS APART
WHEN HE EATS IT!!!—in the toaster.

*

I love Uncle because he wants me to win respect. Once, smack
in the midst of a crisis, my cellphone went dead. I despaired.
Uncle, setting down the paper, gave a yell that rocked the coffee
in our cups.

"I DON'T LIKE TO SEE YOU ACT THAT WAY!!!" I lifted
my face out of my hands. He lowered his voice. "This is what I

learned in the army. If you can handle situations when others are
losing their nerve, others will respect you." (Till then, if I'd had
a watchword, it had not been *Win Respect*. It had been more like
What Now.) I wonder if, on the field of coma, Uncle is winning
purple hearts. Aunt has been Googling his condition and following links anywhere. Dear Aunt who believes her dreams.

*

Tonight, the bathroom faucets keep me awake, turned to a drip
so the pipes don't freeze: *bwupp, bwupp, bwupp.* . . . Overhead, a
hemlock bough breaks: gunshot, crash of ice and kettledrum sub-
sidence. I regard the nightlight, shaped like Jesus spreading his
hands. Which might mean "You're asking me?"

Sleepless, I try to read. Aunt's books are mostly about man-
agement psychology, mindfulness, positivity, those arts of the
troubled American spirit. *Mermaids, Centaurs, Werewolves, and
Dragons: True Myths from Ancient Times* has a cracked spine and
smells of . . . beauty salon. I turn to the chapter on werewolves.
My shadow snores under the blankets and I am very glad he is a
dog, not a wolf. What if my good shepherd were a wolf? Thank
goodness. Yet the author of *Mermaids, Centaurs,* et.al. has an up-
beat view of werewolves. In the records of the Inquisition, tran-
scripts of Latvian men tortured for werewolfery reveal that these
men were faithful Christians.

"We are Christ's dogs," they insisted, refusing to admit traffic
with the devil. "We do battle with the devils," they assured the
holy officers who directed their mutilation. "We go down into
hell and do battle with the devils. We are Christ's dogs." Over and
over, the werewolves of Latvia said who they were, and what they
stood for, with the courage that wins respect. So claims Aunt's
cracking paperback, while nightlight Jesus spreads his polymer
hands, as if summoning his pack.

*

On this somehow ominously sunny day, I'm worried. Is the heat ebbing in the house? Do I feel drafts? I dig out the furnace maintenance instructions, mislaid among the newspapers, and place them by the phone, which instantly rings like a cartoon lightning bolt labeled RING!!!

"He couldn't breathe," Aunt reports, "he got pneumonia. They had to cut a hole in his throat for an air tube." A dove's note in her voice. "He's on, what's it's name, nutrition through the IV."

"Intravenous."

"That's it. He's lost twenty-eight pounds. He looks like somebody out of a concentration camp. The poor guy!" she exclaims. "The surgeon says it's because the neurologist gave him a drug against seizures during the operation but the neurologist says that's normal, actually I didn't talk to the neurologist, just to his resident, and I'm supposed to talk with him—the chief neurologist—but nobody knows when, so I'm waiting."

"Are you dating your notes?" She is. Names, dates, *times.*

"They say, if he pulls through, we have to pay for the ambulance to take him home because Medicare won't cover it. Guess what that costs?"

I know—I've talked to my cousins, her son and daughter, who wanted to drive their parents home but gave up after a few nights at their respective airports. The Eastern seaboard is closed except for military and medical aircraft.

"I'm not paying for an ambulance. After what they did to him?" Aunt sounds more herself. "That's ridiculous." It hurts my eyes to look outside, where the neighbors' BMW peeps above the snow, and a shovel quivers in the wind.

"How's your shadow? Anything new?" My elbows rest on the counter, hips outslung, fitting myself into a sunbeam. Under the counter, my shadow plays on the cabinet.

"He's sniffing the bread drawer."

"Your uncle had a dog, did you know?" I didn't. "His name was Pepper—a mutt. He loved that dog, Pepper. I wonder . . ."

"How could my shadow be the ghost of a dog I never heard of before?"

"Sometimes, I don't know, love takes strange forms."

*

One parent dead, one parent crazy. That's my heritage, by no means unique; and which is a tale of American commonplaces that does not bear repeating to myself in this deepfreeze. Love takes strange forms, like one's own existence.

*

Pepper and I check each room for cold baseboards. In the master bedroom, a taupe blouse trails one sleeve from the wide bed to the floor. I want to cry. It's as if the past were still here, easily retrievable—the rush to pack, this blouse forgotten as Aunt goes downstairs dragging the suitcase, Uncle behind her angrily clutching the bannister.

Turning away, I meet a face—mine—between the mirrored tops of Aunt's perfumes on the dresser. Here's the framed photograph of my grandparents' golden anniversary. My cousins and me, just kids, with arms like macaroni. The wedded pair, Grandfather in his humped suit, Grandmother without a face. Light fell too long on that spot. Grandmother's lilac dress holds the photographer's directed pose, while her face has slipped away.

*

Help! My shadow is pulling me off my feet, towing me into a run! Pepper races downstairs into the kitchen where the phone RINGS!!!, RINGS!!!, and RINGS!!! I lunge for it. No one's on the other line.

Slowly replacing the headset, I see that Pepper has disappeared. I have no shadow. I wave my hand over the sunlit counter. No shadow! Of course, granite doesn't show shadows well. But then I see, *around the corner*, my dog-shadow like an outsize splash of black coffee on the basement door, dilating and contracting as he pants. Light doesn't bend around corners that way. Apparently, darkness does.

No. I'm not going into the basement. I know what's at the bottom of the stairs.

*

To the left, a roomful of cartons. Aunt took me there, recently. She picked her way around the dim storeroom and raised her arms like a dancer, laughing. "Take something! Anything! I don't want the kids to have to clear out all this junk." Boxed china, DVDs, gym equipment, baby clothes. The glass tank where my cousins' pet snake died. (She swore it was empty; I didn't look.) One midcentury lounger shaped like an orange velvet scroll. Speaking as an accountant, I told her the lounger was the only thing worth money.

*

To the right, there's the laundry room and furnace, the ironing board with rusted joints, and sadness in the very air.

*

Pepper paws at the basement doorknob! Scratches! *Barks!* Really, I hear something like the shadow of a bark. I'm not going down there. But I open the door.

The basement stairs are the hell-twin of the attic stairs, mustard-green carpeted with a dirty track down the center of the shaggy risers. I listen. The electric furnace mutters in its Bedlam corner, the original sin of this house, which should have been heated by natural gas, oil, solar, geothermal—anything but a temperamental giant toaster oven in the basement. The furnace isn't evil, quite, but it's a royal pain in the ass. Sternly, I tell Pepper we're not going down there. The heat's still on, isn't it? Be a good boy.

*

Long night, frozen night, universal night it feels like. Tucked under the mounded quilts, I dream that night after night will pass, Uncle will return, night after night will pass, Aunt will nurse him back to health, night after night will pass, summer will come. Towards dawn, I throw an arm over the quilts and yank it back, coated with a scrim of cold. I sit up and a pudding of cold molecules pours down my neck into my pajamas. The air I'm breathing paints my nose, throat and lungs with the same coldness. Diving back under the covers, I pray it's just a low point in the heating cycle. I dream of getting up warm and happy; I dream of realizing that I'm dreaming. When daylight presses through the sheet over my face, I draw it away and breathe nauseating cold.

*

Wearing Aunt's down coat, in every room I find the baseboards cold. Water's still coming from the faucets, but time is running out before the pipes freeze. Pepper paces anxiously, whining and blurting caninisms—*buf! khwuppt!*—while I call every phone number on the emergency list: two electricians and a plumber, the appliance service, Last Resort Handyman, and the neighbors. No one answers. The businesses are closed. I leave voicemails that sound dead on arrival. No choice remains but to read aloud the Electric Furnace Instructions, three yellowed pages in Uncle's vigorous cursive, rattling in my hand. *DO NOT TOUCH EXPOSED WIRES! LOOK FOR LOOSE CONNECTIONS BUT DO NOT TOUCH! CALL FOR HELP INSTEAD.*

*

Stop whining, Pepper. Win respect. It's probably the circuit breaker, and we'll fix it.

*

My shadow paws the basement doorknob. I descend the frigid stairway. Near the bottom, instead of the laundry room's wan light on the cement landing, there is grayish rippling in which the steps are immersed, weedy ledges. Staring down in shock, I hear the lapping stir of Aunt's stored stuff sorting itself into the waters. Out of the dark storeroom floats the orange velvet lounger and rocks gently over the drowned landing. Pepper leaps onto the curved seat, its nap showing through his wagging tail as my arms flail against a misstep that lands me slap on top of him, clinging to the unsteady lounger.

We drift toward the laundry room, abreast a flood loaded with voltage from the furnace's exposed wiring, now submerged.

*

Turning like a clockhand round and round, in the middle of the laundry room, I shift my weight with the lounger's wobbles, clinging hopefully. The circuit breakers are higher than the water. If I can grapple toward the furnace by holding onto a wall, pulling the lounger forward! But the universe does not indulge this notion. I am prone on my fickle raft, chin rubbing mouse shit, trying by shifts of weight to rhyme with the lounger's yawing and dipping, to avoid capsizing by clutch, swing, cling, as my raft revolves, tipsy-topsily, in the middle of the room. Whose grimy windows throw sunlight across the indoor lagoon of electric death.

I glimpse the ironing board fallen over, rust-washed, building up shock potential, as I register the backwards yaw commanding me to counterbalance, and the soft lolloping of ripples as the unit composed of me and mildewed lounger reinvents its relation to the water, drifting round again. From this circle's terror-physics, there must be a drain causing the shallow whirlpool I ride—a floor drain, great, how long until it drains? How long can I keep on balancing? One misstep! One misstep! Whole me reduced to chance! Take it back, this isn't real! I'm not supposed to die here! What a stupid expression in these walls I crave to brace my hands against—as if Aunt were here on a normal day, ironing the laundry, Uncle's shouts bouncing like a monstrous Slinky down the basement stairs. Walls, I know you, don't you know me? Stupid walls, callous walls, oh, dearly beloved walls. It's over.

*

A blur.

*

Urgent questions. Only when I lose the hope of answers—quite against the grain of an accountant—then it appears: blades of grass casting separate shadows, a plain of shadow-grass stretching from clear green stems. How straight each one is, how sure of its mission!

*

As I shift my focus—the way I shifted my body on the lounger before it capsized—a panorama unfolds. Like everything, it takes practice: I learn to shift focus sideways from the blur, toward the grass-roofed houses, the meadow of tufted grasses, the forested mountain sheltering the meadow, and the trails snaking deep into the forest. I see each green tooth in the spiral of a fiddlehead at the trailside. Once I see it all, I can ignore the blur at the center. There is, isn't there, always a blur?

*

First by accident—hey, it's the Library! Then it's gone. I practice how to find the Library again. Shift focus delicately, like sniffing

a scent hidden in the breeze: grass: Library: Library: grass. Between each—grass, Library—comes the central blur, like some
kind of hinge between one meaningful state and another. Now
as I stand sniffing with my mind, an eddy in the air becomes a
security door with a steel push bar.

I stare hard at it. The door responds, in yellow, "RESTRICT-
ED ACCESS." And . . . I don't know what to do. I just don't
know what to do. Wishing Pepper were around, I regard my
shadow—a vague stick figure through which the grass grows.
How I long for the dog who pawed at the basement doorknob.

Perhaps it is my strong longing that brings into view a red torii
gate. Walking through that tall gate, like a child I walk straight
into Grandmother's arms.

*

My heart agog, I tell her, "You look wonderful."

She seems relaxed; her hair and nails are glossy as if she's
been to a spa. It is truly she, gone so long; her face turns slowly
toward me so that I can recover, with each heartbeat, her sweet
known features, even her lips like worn silk ribbons stretched into
a smile.

"You're the one who does all the thinking?" she asks, checking her mental list of descendants. Hiding my face against her,
I confess how I tried to protect the house, but left the basement
flooded with electrified water and my own body on the floor.

Grandmother doesn't smell of sweat or onions as she used to,
but of sachet. She takes my shoulders and holds me in front of
her. "Let me look at you," she says. "Open your eyes. Wider."

And I try.

The periphery around Grandmother fills with the noble vol-
umes of the Library, and those who are studying here. From the
linenfold panels of the walls, from the hanging iron chandeliers,
from the oaken tables, silent music swells. A book opens itself, a
book so enormous that I have to support it with both arms. In
its parchment margins swim, soar, cavort, wriggle, wave, hover,

burrow and entangle the living beasts of the world, drawn in inks of powdered gems and murex. In one square inch, holding my breath, I discover a ruby-throated hummingbird, a cabbage butterfly, a barred owl, zebra mussels, a nudibranch, a shoebill, a spider moth, yellow-crested flycatchers, prairie wolves, an acorn weevil, a purple frog, a vampire squid, a sea hare, a sequined spider, a tiger quoll, a black dragonfish, stinkbugs, mice upon mice, fruit bats, white bats, honeybees, mason bees, a flying fox, and a bone-eating snot flower that feeds only on the sunken bones of whales.

Astounded at their richness and beauty, I see they are alive! The hummingbird stabs a blossom; butterflies flitter and mate; owls ready their talons midair to cage the fleeing mice; mussels sieve the current in their snaggly lips. My arms tremble under the book's weight. The text cannot be read; it slips away as I puzzle over it, the way Grandmother's face slipped away from our family photograph. Yet I catch the gist of its formal splendor and density of meaning, immortal—or the next best thing (my accounting habit notes) since the Sun's days are counted. I look up from the pages groaning and humming with life, and Grandmother is waiting for me.

"I want to know my mission," I whisper.

*

With these words, the Library, the wonderful Library, is gone. My urgent question has thrown me back into the blur, where the only comfort is in clasping Grandmother's hand as I did when I was small and had to cross the street. The blur is total. Shifting focus does no good. My body's crumbling into separate parts, centrifuged into fog. I can't shout, my mouth is gone. My hand with Grandmother's in it is a wind-snatched kite without a string. The fog's streaked with dark specks, flying sideways like snow, but the thickening specks are not snow—actually, it's seeds! Shiny black seeds with pink spots; pink seeds with black spots, not falling, but held in a slow spin that resembles a migration of living creatures—sardines in a swirling funnel, locusts in a revolving swarm—or spheres of rain packed in a turning cyclone. I'm travelling with a storm of seeds.

Suddenly I find that I am perched on the storm's inner wall, a curved slope of immeasurable extent down which the mass of black-pink, pink-black seeds dwindles, obedient to perspective, toward an abyss out of whose bottomless pinkish-gray haze something rises: a figure that dominates all that distance, shrinking it, paralyzing thought with awe. The figure is arrayed in seeds of infinite shapes and sizes, in every color from the basalt-flow rumbling of infrared to the keening of radioactive violet. At a great height, the figure's head—the back of its head—emerges in a neon pink, helmet-shaped wig. The oscillation of the figure's robed back suggests an arm performing some type of careful handiwork. I'm small as an atom, infinitely smaller than the coruscating, pink-wigged form, which rotates very slowly, like the axis of the universe.

*

It's all here, I realize. Here is everything that exists. Every star and meteor, every newborn and skeleton, every whole and broken thing. My orange lounger is here somewhere. And the houseplants. Aunt and Uncle are here without knowing it. Her taupe blouse. And the snow, the polar vortex snow, the snow in all its frightful tonnage. In some incomprehensible way they are all here, cheek by jowl, seed beside seed; and I hear Grandmother sigh with longing.

"What are you looking for?" I ask, since it's clear she's trying to spot something special in the immensities.

"My cash drawer," she replies; and after pausing, tells me a story. As a young girl, Grandmother worked in a bargain basement full of women hunting for marked-down clothes. It could get rowdy: once, she'd had to separate two customers going at it with screams, curses, and a designer bridal gown stretched to the tearing point between their nails. When she returned to her register, the cash drawer was gone. The store manager docked the missing cash from her last paycheck, fired her, and called her a thief.

"I have never heard this story?" I say.

"I was ashamed, honey girl," Grandmother whispers. "I couldn't tell nobody."

(Slowly, as this pair of atoms converses, the Figure's cheek comes into view, big as a harvest moon.)

"The store was insured," I reply. "Those bastards had no right to dock your pay."

"So ashamed," Grandmother sighs, and death has not absolved her. "I shouldn't have turned my back."

*

Oh it is here. Proof of all wrongs, lies and cruelty. All here— the receipts. And for so long, I've placed my faith in numbers that cannot lie. I believed that accountability counted. But now, you know, I am just pissed off. I want to avenge Grandmother's shame. I want to rescue Uncle from the strutting experts who promise, bungle, and hide. I want to save Aunt's head from the basement wall. I want to save Grandfather, Uncle's model, from the poverty that forced him to leave school, so that ever after he itched to hurl his family's heads at the wall. I want to save my parents from insanity and death. I want to save myself. It infuriates me. It is all here! The proof, the incontrovertible evidence, the arguments Uncle would make in the name of justice. *Haa? Haa?* HAA?!

*

The Figure has rotated to show its tremendous face, golden as a South Sea pearl. An old, heavy-jowled face. Its experienced lips, loose and full, are lipstick crimson. Beneath its straight pink bangs and crooked black eyebrows, the eyes hold an expression that might have been human before our race began to speak; but on second glance, those are not mortal eyes. Its hand moves too swiftly to see, even in the slowed-down time that we inhabit; that hand must move much faster than light, I think. From the drape and flow of the seed-raiment, it seems the hand is engaged in fine brushwork. At third glance, the demeanor of the Figure is modest and animated with gentle fervor, inviting beauty. Beauty steals through me, infinite beauty remaking all that terror has undone.

"God," calls Grandmother, cajoling, "my grandchild has a question."

*

My question puts God at a disadvantage, I sense. The black-browed, pink-coiffed face is as mute as if those oceanic red lips were nothing. God cannot understand what a question *is*. God has neither incompleteness nor longing for completeness. God is translated entirely into action, into glorious painting, without desire, curiosity or thought, much less second thought. Yet I am in the painting, Grandmother is in the painting, and the many-colored seed-robe winds God into the painting too, as God paints the expanding storm of the universe. God's great cheek cannot host a tear, which, were it to fall, would collapse everything, and God would sleep, and nothing would happen. . . .

God's small voice says, *Go back. Go to hell.*

*

RING!!! RING!!! RING!!! RING!!!

*

Up the basement stairs to grab the phone. My cold coat's waterlogged, slab feet slip in sopped shoes, the ice skeleton wearing my wet flesh shakes and shakes. Teeth a-rattle, electrified with cold, I juggle the headset. It's Last Resort Handyman, returning my call.

"You're tellin' *me*. There ain't a house in this neighborhood without a couple feet of water in the cellar. All from the storm sewer, nothin' we can do, it's the city's problem. Goin' out the drain? Good. We gotta to get your furnace on, and in my experience, Arnie's furnace, I musta told him fifty times to *keep that flame sensor clean*, save his wife the trouble of callin' me every time. But he don't do it. Your uncle's a great guy, I love him, but he's his own boss. I'm sorry he's in the hospital. That's hard. You all right?"

"Mm-my teeth are ch-ch-ch-ch . . ."

"Oh boy. Jump up and down and wave your arms, I'll wait."

". . . Thanks. The doors are blocked, nobody can get in."

"You got a smartphone, I'll walk you through it. Sure. Arnie's niece, Arnie's family, anything I can do. Course, if it *ain't* the flame sensor, *then* we may have a problem."

*

I squeak out of soaked clothes, pull on dry clothes, boots—fast as I can, shivering like a leaf—and call Handyman on Facetime. I'm worried he won't exist, but he does, and his nut-sized face tells me to get a screwdriver. Can't find one anywhere. From the oracle's cave of my palm, Handyman's voice tells me what to fetch instead.

"A dollar?" I echo. "A butter knife?"

*

Four screws to be unscrewed with the tip of a butter knife. The cover comes off the furnace, and there, coyly, on a steel ledge behind a skein of wires, lies a screwdriver. Choking, Handyman says that Uncle should stick to law. I hold up my phone for him to see the three burner pipes. Turn the power on, he orders. I flip the power switch. The burner pipes now culminate in three glowing, orange culverts. The gas valve clicks open!—but the cheer dies on my lips, the fire dies, the furnace stops dead.

Handyman shouts to turn the power off. I do that. The screwdriver comes in handy as I twist a single screw head flush with the deep wall of the furnace. With numb fingers, I extract a pipe no thicker than a dragon's whisker, with a ninety-degree bend. The flame sensor. I follow orders and take a dollar from my pocket.

"Fold the dollar around the flame sensor and rub it clean," Handyman says.

"Which side do I use?"

"Don't matter, just pretend like it's Scotch-Brite," he urges.

In a cold minute I've rubbed the pipelet to a sheen with the face of my country's father, pretending he's a cleaning pad. And when I restart the furnace, it stays on, motor swooshing, triple pipes of its heart aglow. Handyman's mini-face wrinkles merrily, his eyebrows bounce up, he doesn't mind a check by the end of the month. When he vanishes from my palm, I'm sad; it's so long since I talked with a person's face. But the furnace is muttering benisons and the house, the house is saved.

*

I pocket my phone. The laundry room feels as vacant as a drained swimming pool. Finally, in the wan light, I see Aunt's orange lounger lying on its side. The flood's remnants pour calmly into the floor drain that seems ringed by glass. What a shipwreck, I think, pondering the lounger. Plastered over its curved frame, muddy swathes are ribbed with orange creases; the ruined folds are somehow articulate, as if soaked with a soul. Now I recall that spinning ride, how scared I was. And the flood never reached the wiring! But when did everything happen? Counting back, it seems that I was unconscious for about an hour. I had capsized, right. . . . In God's name, how had I not drowned?

The question holds me, listening to the furnace's utterance and the whispery gurgle of the drain. I can't remember. My guess is that after capsizing, I waded over to the stairs and collapsed. I got into this mess by chance, and out of it by luck. There's something missing, though . . . something, something.

On impulse, I grab the lounger and try to right it, but the spongy fabric makes a retching sound, and splits. Later, I'll do repairs. Satisfied that the past events are generally accounted for, weak with fatigue, I leave the laundry room.

*

But the stairs give me pause: they're as soggy as boiled spinach. Maybe I can bring a hair dryer down here with a super-long extension cord, I muse; and glancing into the storeroom to guess the whereabouts of a wall socket, I get a shock. Deep in the dimness, surrounded by cartons immemorial, stands . . . Aunt's orange velvet lounger.

*

This is unaccountable. On my palms, I see orange smears from tugging at the lounger *in the laundry room*. There are not two loungers.

*

I retrace my steps to the laundry room. The furnace mutters, the floor drain rests in its glassy halo. The lounger is gone. Nowhere. Wandering stupidly, I trip over the ironing board, and wrench its screeching legs upright. What I saw, knew, and touched with my own hands, I somehow didn't see, know, or touch. I could weep, trudging back. Please let it be a mistake. But it's not a mistake. It's Aunt's lounger in the dusky storeroom. Surrounded by cartons no one has moved in years.

As my vision adjusts to the dimness, those cartons look— half-melted. Their corners are soft. Their sides sag. There's a cardboard box on the threshold, at my feet, and when I raise its flap, the wet flap comes off. Wet cardboard in hand, I have a vision of the future. I see a Stygian cloud of black mold blanketing all the things in Aunt's storeroom. No one will be able to live with

that. And I know my mission: every last thing in that haunted
storeroom will have to be cleaned, by hand, by me.

*

I am putting the butter knife in the dishwasher when Aunt calls.

"He woke up today." Oh! "He's out of it, mentally. He doesn't
know me." Ah.

I lean both elbows on the counter, gazing into its granite
mirror.

"They think his brain could recover, they're saying . . . we have
to wait. If he doesn't make progress in the next two weeks, they
say it's probably for life."

"He'll be okay." But how glib, when it's not me sitting at Uncle's bedside as the IV and catheter drip, Aunt covers his wracked
hand with her own, and his mind's doors slam open, slam shut, in
the highest wind of all.

"How's your shadow, still a dog?" In the shadow of my bulky
sweats, I spot a tail tip.

"He's hiding. It's cloudy today. Listen, do you have some
heavy-duty rubber gloves?"

"Under the sink. What for?"

"I may do a little cleaning up in the basement. Just, like, ah, do
something useful with my time." During the pause, I hear Aunt
addressing muffled courtesies to the CNA who's come for Uncle's
bloodwork. Then her voice bursts out like a bold fragrance.

"Are you crazy? You're crazy! What's the point of—do I
have to tell you? If I was single like you, know where I'd be
now? *Mexico.*" My impression is that Aunt has risen to her feet.
"Why don't you do something nice? You've got the whole place
to yourself. Enjoy it! Take a bubble bath! Watch movies! Call
your old boyfriends, ask how the weather's treating them, why
not? Bake some brownies, there's recipes in that tea tin," she
points out; and the cajoling tone in her voice stops her, as it
has since she first, how long ago, began putting an automatic
smile in her voice.

"You are right," I allow. "I'll test the recipes and make brownies for when you come home."

"Put pot in them," she jokes. "Now that pot is legal, I should try it."

*

After talking with Aunt, the house feels like home again. The toaster oven exudes its odor of good bread, and the tomato soup its savor. The radio speaks calmly of our calamities. I'm too tired for TV. When I go to bed, nightlight Jesus spreads a glow of welcome, blessing the warmth that crepitates in the attic walls. I lie awake composing a protocol. (1) Remove boxes, one at a time, from the storeroom. (2) Throw the wet cardboard in trash bags. Clean and dry the boxes' contents. (3) Once the storeroom is empty, clean the exercise machines, mop the floor, let dry, and replace the cleaned items. (4) WIN RESPECT. Mentally I erase the last item, because, as Aunt knows, no one wins respect for housecleaning, even in a haunted basement.

*

In the morning, on the soggy basement steps, I know that nothing is haunted. If Pepper looks like a creeping mound of risen hackles, that's because he's just a dog. I kneel among cartons, their sides streaked and furrowed as the wet digests them from the bottom up. I pull the nearest box, but it slumps, and—like an abdomen rupturing in the coroner's hands—releases its contents, a pile of baby clothes. Pepper sniffs at the tiny jerseys that Aunt couldn't part with. I throw the lot, fluttering like baby ghosts, into the washing machine (luckily still working) in the other room. As I dismantle more cartons, kneeling in puddles, the clothes stretch into childhood. So far, so good, I tell Pepper without opening my lips. The usual basement smells—dust, damp, fabric softener—have curdled into something I don't want in my mouth. Yet when I unpack the twelve-place dinner service inherited from my grandparents, stacked like vertebrae in decomposed cartons, my mouth fills with the memory of bone broth. I hold the white tureen that once hovered before me in Grandmother's hands, fluted all round like a classical temple. Long after her death, Grandfather cried for her bone broth. But what I hold now, before my heart, is a cheap crock, no more made of porcelain (as I'd believed) than of pearl from the seas of the moon.

I lug the old dishware, and the cousins' Marvel-themed juice glasses, and the rest, by stages into the kitchen and run the dishwasher. Meanwhile, there's a box of bristling naked dolls. (Bucket of soapy water.) And a box of stuffed animals infested with moth larvae. (Sadly, trash bag.) I sponge crud off a dozen DVDs. I wipe vinyl records with cleanser till they gleam like geisha hair and dry the album covers. The farther I go, the filthier the wet floor is, until it oozes black from a tangled clump of chains like something out of a dungeon. Swallowing hard, I prod the clump with my boot and surprise a clatter of enormous teardrops. Oh, woe! This is the Argentinian chandelier, my grandparents' pride, whose crystals, turning in splendor, depended from branches above our heads whenever the family sat down to a holiday feast! And has it fallen so? Has it lain the years through, tarnishing into this.

*

Opening a box of maps: the roads are fungal threads, the towns are mildew blooms. Equal damage to top and bottom suggests a gradual decay, like this insane winter fed by carbon emissions through years of family drives. I hate to dump maps, but do it, holding my breath as mold billows in the trash bag. Then I smell something. Pepper, ears alert, spreads himself thin over the cartons, clearing—with a fusillade of snorts that make me jump—his nasal apparatus. He's louder than anything since the phone rang; and looking hard, I perceive that the snorts come not from Pepper, but from underneath him, in the middle of the room. Something gigantic chokes for air through an obstacle. Pray God the *other* sewer isn't backing up!

I high-step over the remaining boxes and ram both knees—
yelling with pain—against the tank in which my cousins' pet
snake died.

*

Unluckily, the tank's walls were higher than the flood. So far, I've
ignored the thin stew of insect parts that my baggy-kneed sweats
absorb as I sit unpacking. That seems natural. It's not the same
as the big glass tank, from whose corners sags a cobweb loomed
in wooly Hell. Loud snorts, under the tank, are shaking this vile
fabric. In the distance, Pepper's barks become frantic. I lean my
weight against the tank and budge it off another floor drain, in
which dark sludge is panting. As I choke on shit-lily stench, gag-
ging my very soul, I'm raised off my feet and tilted backward,
under pressure like an astronaut during acceleration.

Pinned in midair, staring into two red orbs, I see countless
scales graduating down in size from prison-yard paving stones, to
back-alley cobbles, to sewer tiles around the double pits of serpent nostrils. The lights are out. The jaws begin to crank apart,
eclipsing those red eyes. There are no teeth; Hell is time, digest-
ing me headfirst. I strain but cannot move, while a ringing noise
swings through each moment. Down into my eyes, which cannot
shut, lowers an enormous, luminous anatomy of pulpy tissues
and palatal ridges running with saliva.

I cannot fight, I cannot save this house.

*

Shift focus. Losing the mind is the last freedom. Lose it, and
glimpse—radiant in the blur of guttering thought—the golden
apples of the west, Aunt's orange velvet lounger, that unfurls
from its dark corner and flies toward me on wings of flame.

*

Always a central blur, isn't there. On one side, a storm sewer serpent and an orange fire dragon, fighting.

On the other side, a human brain, self-playing Theremin, its quirings and eerie scales reestablishing themselves till a sphere of electrochemical music surrounds that bruised, shaven head; and Uncle looks straight at Aunt from the hospital bed, and his lips form her name.

*

The first batch of brownies goes fast. Pepper leaps for shadow-walnuts that I toss into the batter. As the brownies bake, he sprawls by the warm oven. It's a windy day; between gusts, I hear a moan of dog contentment. I'm so hungry that when the phone RINGS!!!, I squeeze the headset between ear and shoulder while licking the spatula.

"He's getting it back," Aunt reports in the bland tone of endurance. "He's going to be okay, in his mind. But his, what's it called, I'm so tired, the tube the food goes down, I'm forgetting words I've known all my life."

"Esophagus?"

"His esophagus. It's paralyzed. He has to eat through a stomach tube. I'll have to give him his meals that way."

I drop the spatula. "Won't it wear off, eventually?"

"They say it's forever, but I'm going to try acupuncture. There's a lot of alternative medicine out there that these so-called experts don't know a thing about." Aunt's voice fills with inventive dreams.

"How's he taking it?"

"Pretty good. He's glad to be alive. He's mad at the doctors."

"Giving them the works?"

"He can't. He can only whisper because of what happened in his throat." Aunt and I hear each other's somber smiles.

I can't help thinking of Aunt tied to Uncle through the umbilicus of his stomach tube, needing her constant care. Is that one of love's strange forms? Will she ever travel back to Mexico?

*

Three days of toil, this took me. I take a last stroll through the storeroom, checking out the clean dishware, the record albums weighted to prevent warping, the folded clothes, the donation-ready dolls. In the laundry room, salvaged family photos are pinned to a clothesline.

Here's Aunt in her bridal gown, and a four-year-old girl holding her hands, gazing all the way up that slope of glazed satin. We're dancing, I remember. Aunt looked as beautiful as the sky. Everything here is cared for, that's the point. My cousins will never hear the last of their hellish snake tank, where I fainted from sheer horror or low blood sugar—maybe the latter, I had no appetite for three days. On the other hand, I'll spare my cousins; their father's situation is hard enough. I'll just ask Aunt if I can have the lounger.

That relic of the seventies is the only thing in here I haven't moved or cleaned. From time to time, I visit its dim corner and admire its dramatic form: no legs or pedestal, a pure scrolling in space. Despite the water damage, its plush color still smolders through grime and shadows. Sometimes I'm tempted to look for the rip I left in the upholstery. I turn into a hunched-over obsessive, peering here, peering there, fists clenched on the memory of orange smears. Too much remains unaccountable. But a prolonged search makes me sneeze, and with tears of mixed character running out my nose, I flee the basement, Pepper sprinting beside me. My relation to Aunt's lounger is vexed. Yet it's worth money, and I'd like to get it professionally restored. I find myself wanting to possess it, the very shape of an unanswerable question, on which I would like to stretch out, someday, and reflect.

ACKNOWLEDGMENTS

In writing this book, I had the assistance of some very generous scientists and friends. Heartfelt thanks go to Dr. Moira van Staaden, professor of biological sciences at Bowling Green State University, who supplied innumerable useful links about genomics and cichlids, patiently answered endless questions, and helped me glimpse the inner life of those who, in seeking nature's truth, are never surprised to be surprised by it. Thanks are also due to Dr. Aaron Gitler, director of Gitler Lab at Stanford University, for an informative lab tour and excellent advice; Dr. Alya Rachel Raphael, for sharing her fascinating work at Gitler Lab; Dr. Alexis Mychajliw, for explaining the perspective of field biologists and showing me the actual skeleton in Stanford's closet; Dr. Marcus Feldman, director of the Morrison Institute for Population and Resource Studies at Stanford University, for an intellectually gripping lunch; and Dr. Mark Kaganovitch, CEO of SolveBio, for philosophically profound remarks about genomics. To David Schlapbach, Manhattanite extraordinaire, I am grateful for invaluable tips about the habits of the global business elite. Peter Ullman kindly provided an insider's insight into the culture of Silicon Valley. My husband, Tom, let me read drafts aloud over dinner and gave loving support.

Finally, the presiding spirit of this book is that of my late friend and mentor, Diane Wood Middlebrook, whose voice I continue to hear.

I would also like to acknowledge the publications in which many of these stories originally appeared:

"Menu: Extinction" in *Granta*, Vol 117, Autumn 2011

"The Bath of Venus" in *Stand*, Vol 18(3), 2020

"Bedcrumbs" in *Puerto Del Sol,* Vol 53, Spring 2018

"Animal Truth" Part 1, in *Eclectica,* April/May 2020

"Animal Truth" Part 2, titled "Lucky Animal" in *About Place,* Vol V, Issue IV, 2020